"How dare you?"
Joanna could hardly speak

Cal Blackstone threw back his head and laughed. "Said in the manner born," he mocked. "The well-bred young lady rebuking the upstart pleb."

"I refuse to listen to any more of this."

"You don't have to." Cal was infuriatingly at ease. "I want you and I'm going to have you. There's nothing more to be said."

"Well, you couldn't be more wrong!" Joanna flung the words at him, trying to keep her voice steady. "I have a few things to say myself and the first is that I wouldn't have you, Callum Blackstone, if you came gift-wrapped."

"And what do you know about it?" he asked softly, still smiling. "What do you know about anything, Miss Chalfont, except pride and your own version of the past?"

SARA CRAVEN probably had the ideal upbringing for a budding writer. She grew up by the seaside in a house crammed with books, a box of old clothes to dress up in and a swing outside in a walled garden. She produced the opening of her first book at age five and is eternally grateful to her mother for having kept a straight face. Now she has more than twenty-five novels to her credit. The author is married and has two children.

Books by Sara Craven

HARLEQUIN PRESENTS

1119—COMPARATIVE STRANGERS
1143—DEVIL AND THE DEEP SEA
1176—KING OF SWORDS
1241—ISLAND OF THE HEART
1279—FLAWLESS
1330—STORM FORCE

SARA CRAVEN

when the devil drives

Harlequin Books

TORONTO • NEW YORK • LONDON
AMSTERDAM • PARIS • SYDNEY • HAMBURG
STOCKHOLM • ATHENS • TOKYO • MILAN
MADRID • WARSAW • BUDAPEST • AUCKLAND

Harlequin Presents first edition July 1992
ISBN 0-373-11471-0

Original hardcover edition published in 1991
by Mills & Boon Limited

WHEN THE DEVIL DRIVES

CHAPTER ONE

'Simon, you don't—you can't mean this! It's a joke, isn't it—one of your appalling, tasteless bloody jokes?'

Simon Chalfont's face reddened, and his glance shifted away from the anguished appeal in his sister's eyes.

'I'm totally serious, old girl.' He sighed. 'God, Jo, if I could change things, I would. But you weren't here, and the bank wouldn't lift a finger to help me. I was desperate.'

'So you've mortgaged us—this house—the workshop—the little we have left—to Cal Blackstone.' Joanna Bentham's hands gripped the back of the chair as if it were the only reality in a suddenly tottering world. 'I can't believe it. I can't credit that you'd do such a thing.'

'And what was I supposed to do?' Simon demanded defensively. 'Lay the men off? Close the workshop? Try and sell this house?'

'If you were so strapped for cash, surely there are other sources you could have borrowed from in the short term?'

'A loan shark, perhaps,' Simon suggested derisively. 'For God's sake, Jo, do you know the kind of interest those people charge?'

'I know the kind of interest Cal Blackstone could charge.' Joanna drew a shaky breath. 'Simon, don't you realise what you've done? You've sold us lock, stock and barrel to our greatest enemy!'

'Oh, I knew that was coming.' Simon flung himself on to the sofa, giving his sister a trenchant look. 'Don't you think it's time we grew up and forgot all about this ridiculous family feud? Isn't carrying the thing into a third generation going over the top?'

'Ask Cal Blackstone,' Joanna bit back at him. 'He hasn't forgotten a thing. Fifteen years ago, his father took the mill away from us. Now his son's coming for the rest. And, thanks to you, he hasn't even had to fight for it.'

There was a sullen silence.

Joanna released her grip on the chairback, rubbing almost absently the indentations the heavily carved wood had left in her flesh.

Cal Blackstone, she thought, and her skin crawled. The grandson of the man who was once glad to work for my grandfather as an overlooker at the mill. The trouble-maker, the rabble-rouser who tried to close our doors with strikes over and over again. The self-made millionaire who drove Chalfonts to the edge of bankruptcy, and died swearing he'd put us out on the street.

Even after the fierce old man had gone, there was no respite for the beleaguered mill. His son Arnold had proved just as inimical, just as determined. In the end Chalfonts had had to be sold, and there was only one bidder.

Arnold Blackstone got it for a song, Joanna thought, anger welling up inside her. Chalfonts, who'd been making quality worsteds on that site for over a

hundred years. And he made it a byword for ch
rubbish, aimed at the bottom end of the market.

The only thing remaining from the old days wa
the name—Chalfonts Mill—kept deliberately by the
Blackstones, Joanna's father had said bitterly, as a
permanent thorn in the family's flesh—a constant and
public reminder of what they'd lost.

Now, under the direction of Cal Blackstone, his
grandfather's namesake, the mill, as such, no longer
existed. The looms had been sold, and the workforce
dispersed, and the vast building had become a thriving
complex of small industrial workshops and businesses.

Because Cal Blackstone wasn't interested in quality
or tradition. He was an entrepreneur, a developer of
property and ideas. Local gossip said there was hardly
a pie in a radius of two hundred miles that he didn't
have a finger in. And what he touched invariably
turned to gold, Joanna reflected, wincing inwardly.
He'd already more than doubled the fortune his father
and grandfather had left, and at thirty-three years of
age it was reckoned his career had barely even started.

To the outrage of the local landowners, he'd ac-
quired Craigmoor House and its park, which had been
derelict for years, renovated it completely, and, in the
face of strenuous opposition, turned it into a country
club, with an integral restaurant and casino, and a
challenging nine-hole golf course in the reclaimed
grounds.

Within a year, all those who'd been most vocifer-
ously outspoken against the plan were among the
club's most stalwart members.

But the Chalfonts were not among them. Since the
original breach between the first Callum Blackstone

Jonas Chalfont, all those years ago, the families
d never knowingly met under the same roof. The
halfonts had let it be known that they would accept
no invitations which had also been extended to any
member of the Blackstone clan, and the rule had been
rigorously applied by Cecilia Chalfont, Joanna's
mother, who came from an old county family and
carried considerable social clout.

The two families had still been at daggers drawn
when Cecilia had died from an unexpected heart condition while Joanna was in her early teens.

I'm almost glad, Joanna thought fiercely, walking
to the window and staring down at the formal rose
garden, glowing with summer bloom, which it over-
looked. At least Mother was spared the knowledge of
this—betrayal by Simon. But keeping it from Dad will
be another matter.

Anthony Chalfont had his own suite of rooms on
the first floor. Severely crippled by arthritis, he rarely
ventured forth from them, but was looked after de-
votedly by his manservant Gresham, and Joanna's
own elderly nanny.

Just recently, her father's mind had begun to
wander, and he seemed to prefer to dwell very much
in the past. A couple of times since her return, Joanna
had found herself being addressed by him as Cecilia,
although she could see little resemblance in herself to
her mother's haughty beauty. But there were other
days too when his brain was as sharp and lucid as it
had ever been. If Cal Blackstone turned them out of
their home, the effect on her father might be
disastrous.

She took a deep breath. 'Tell me again—slowly—what happened. How you came to do this thing. After all, when I went away the workshop seemed to be doing well. The order-book was full.'

'It was.' Simon's shoulders were hunched, his whole attitude despondent. 'Then everything started to go wrong. Two of our biggest customers gave us backword. They said the recession was biting, and the property market was going into decline. They reckoned people weren't prepared to spend that kind of money on handcrafted furniture and kitchens any more. We were left with thousands of pounds' worth of specially designed gear on our hands.'

'And what about our partner, Philip the super-salesman?' Joanna asked. 'What was he doing about all this?'

Simon shrugged. 'Philip tried to find other markets, but the answer was always the same. Property development was being cut back, and prices kept down. They wanted mass-market stuff people could afford in their show houses.'

Joanna bit her lip hard. It was Philip who'd urged expansion, she thought angrily. Philip who'd persuaded Simon to take on more men, and buy more machinery to fulfil a demand he was confident he could create. In vain, she'd argued that small was beautiful, that they should concentrate on quality rather than quantity, and feel their way cautiously for a while until their markets were firmly established.

But Simon hadn't wanted to listen. He'd wanted to make money fast, and restore the shaky Chalfont fortunes. He'd also wanted to marry Philip's pretty sister

Fiona, so anything Philip suggested was all right with him.

And at first their growth had been meteoric, just as Philip had predicted. Simon and Fiona had been married with all the appropriate razzmatazz, and the couple had moved into Chalfont House. The Craft Company had continued to flourish, and, although Joanna's instincts had still warned her that they should be cautious, she was having deep problems of her own, and her involvement in the business was becoming less and less.

I should have stayed here after Martin died, she thought with a small silent sigh. I shouldn't have run away like that. But I felt I needed time—to lick my wounds—to try and heal myself. There were too many memories here. Too much I needed to forget.

Her headlong flight, after her husband's funeral, had taken her to her godmother's home in the United States. Aunt Vinnie had extended the invitation in a warmly affectionate letter of condolence as soon as she'd heard about Martin's fatal car accident. Joanna hadn't planned on staying more than a few weeks in New Hampshire, but had become interested in spite of herself in the running of the art gallery Aunt Vinnie owned. She'd started helping out for a few hours each week, but had soon grown more deeply involved, and gradually her stay had extended into months.

If her godmother hadn't reluctantly decided to sell up and retire to California, she had to admit she might still have been there.

Clearly, eighteen months had been a long time to absent herself. Too long, she castigated herself.

'We had suppliers to pay, and the wages bill to meet,' Simon went on. 'Things were looking really black. The bank refused outright to allow us to exceed our stated overdraft. In fact, they started pressing us to repay some of it. Jo—I didn't know where to turn.'

She didn't look at him. She continued to stare rigidly down into the garden. 'So you turned to Cal Blackstone. Why?'

'It wasn't quite like that.' The defensiveness was back in his voice. 'He approached me. He was the guest speaker at the Round Table dinner, and the people I was with asked him to join us afterwards for a drink. I couldn't very well avoid him. We were left on our own, and at first he just—made conversation.'

'But later?' Joanna asked matter-of-factly.

'Later—he began to talk about the Craft Company. He seemed to know we were in trouble. He said that things were generally difficult for small businesses, and mentioned a few of the problems some of them were having at Chalfont Mill. He said he'd been able to help in a lot of cases. That it would be a pity to go under, if a simple injection of cash could save the day.'

'Cal Blackstone, philanthropist.' Joanna gave a mirthless laugh. 'And you fell for it!'

Simon came to stand beside her. 'What else was I supposed to do?' he almost hissed. 'Things were bad and getting worse every day. Our creditors were pressing, and the bank was threatening to bounce the wages cheque. If someone offers you a lifeline, you don't throw it back in his face, for God's sake.' He paused. 'Besides, Fiona had just told me she was pregnant.'

With her usual immaculate sense of timing, Joanna thought resignedly. 'So how much did you borrow from him?'

'Twenty thousand to begin with. The rest, later.'

'Using your power of attorney from Dad to put this house up as collateral, I suppose.'

'We had to do something,' Simon said stiffly. 'And Phil's flat is only rented.'

'Lucky Philip! I hope he's got a spare room. You and Fiona are probably going to need it. And the baby when it arrives, of course,' she added, her mouth twisting. 'Have you warned your wife she may shortly be homeless? Not to mention Dad, of course.'

Simon looked at her uneasily. 'Why should it come to that?'

'Because—to quote the words from his letter of today's date—Mr Blackstone wishes to meet you to discuss the extent of your liabilities to him.' She was silent for a moment, then said abruptly, 'He's closing in for the kill, Si. He means to finish what his father and grandfather began. The old man swore he'd see our family on its knees when Grandpa fired him, and turned him out of his cottage all those years ago. Cal Blackstone means to fulfil that pledge.' She shook her head. 'It's as well I came back when I did. I would have hated to return and find all my clothes and other possessions dumped outside on the lawn by the present Mrs Blackstone.' She paused again. 'I presume there is one by now?'

'No one official,' Simon said moodily. 'He's apparently still quite happy to play the field, lucky bastard.'

Joanna bit her lip. She had only been at home for a week, but it was already clear to her that Fiona was not enjoying her pregnancy, and resentment of her condition was making her querulous and demanding. Joanna, torn between the amusement and irritation which her blonde, brainless sister-in-law usually aroused in her, had decided immediately that the prudent course would be to leave the couple to paddle their own rather shaky canoe in privacy.

She had just made arrangements to view a cottage which had come on to the market in the neighbouring valley when Simon had dropped his bombshell about Cal Blackstone's loan.

Blind instinct told her to proceed with her own plans. To walk away from Simon and the mess he'd created, and let him sort it out for himself, while she began to rebuild her life at a safe distance from Chalfont House, the mill, and everything and everyone concerned with it.

But it wasn't as simple as that. Simon had been hard hit by Cecilia's death, and although Joanna was four years his junior she'd learned, in its aftermath, to mother him with almost fierce protectiveness. She couldn't simply abandon him to his fate now.

The dizzy Fiona would be no help, she thought ruefully, totally preoccupied as she was by nausea and vague aches and pains all over her body. And Joanna was still a partner in the Craft Company, although admittedly she'd taken little active part in the running of the business since her marriage.

She had forgotten Simon's propensity for taking the easy way out of any difficulty, she thought, with an inward sigh.

'So when are you planning to see him?' she asked quietly.

'He's coming here tomorrow afternoon.'

'Here?' Joanna stared at him, appalled. 'Why not at the Craft Company?'

Simon shrugged, his expression pettish. 'It wasn't my choice. When I telephoned him, his secretary simply gave me the appointment. There was no consultation about it. She just told me what time he'd be arriving.'

'I can believe it,' Joanna said grimly.

It was the first time a Blackstone had ever set foot in Chalfont House, she realised with a sense of shock. And, if there was anything she could do, it would also be the last.

She said, 'We'll have to try and fend him off, Simon.'

'How?'

Joanna considered for a minute. 'Well—Martin left me some money, not all that much, admittedly, but it's a start, and there's the commission Aunt Vinnie paid me at the gallery. I saved most of it. If we can keep him at bay for a few weeks with that, we might be able to raise the rest of the capital elsewhere.'

'Do you think I haven't tried?' He shook his head. 'I've done everything I can think of. I tell you, Jo, it's hopeless.'

'No!' Joanna said fiercely. 'There is hope—there's got to be. He's not going to take everything away from us.'

'Perhaps he doesn't want to,' Simon suggested hopefully. 'You are rather taking his intentions for granted, you know. Condemning him without a hearing.'

Joanna gave him a level look. 'I have no illusions about Cal Blackstone, or his intentions.' She glanced at her watch. 'Isn't it time you were getting off to the workshop?'

'Hell, yes. But I'd better pop up and see Fiona first. She didn't have a particularly good night.'

Poor old Si, Joanna thought as her brother left the room, his brow furrowed with anxiety. Fiona's vagaries were just one more problem for him to worry over. Troubles never seemed to come singly these days.

She moved over to the sofa and plumped up the cushions which Simon had crushed. As she straightened, she looked up at the big portrait of Jonas Chalfont which hung over the ornate mantelpiece. A harsh face looked down at her, its expression arrogant and dominating, thick grey brows drawn together over his beak of a nose.

She took a breath. The portrait had been painted in her grandfather's heyday, when the Chalfont family were a force to be reckoned with in the Yorkshire woollen industry. Master of all he surveyed, she thought wryly, studying the sitter's proud stance.

It had been soon after the portrait had been finished, however, that Jonas had sacked Callum Blackstone following a violent argument, and evicted him and his small son from their tied cottage. Holding the frightened child in his arms, as bailiffs dumped their possessions into the street, Callum had publicly sworn revenge.

'As you've taken from me, Jonas Chalfont, I'll take from you,' he'd declared, standing bareheaded in the rain. 'Aye, by God, down to every last stick and stone!'

And nothing's gone right for us since, Joanna thought wearily. Oh, Grandfather, you didn't know what you were starting.

Know your enemy, had been one of Jonas's favourite maxims, but he had totally underestimated his former overlooker's sheer force of will and determination to succeed. Just as Simon had failed to assess Cal Blackstone's deviousness of purpose in offering to help the Craft Company financially.

But then Si had never taken the family feud too seriously anyway, Joanna recalled.

'Isn't it time we started to live and let live?' he'd demanded angrily when Joanna had flatly refused to attend a dinner party to which Cal Blackstone had also been invited.

'Not as far as I'm concerned,' Joanna had returned with a toss of her tawny hair. 'If people invite that man, they needn't bother to ask me as well.'

But, as she'd grown up, she'd found it was well-nigh impossible to avoid Cal completely. The Chalfonts were no longer the powerful social mentors they'd once been, and Cal, single, wealthy and darkly attractive, was a welcome visitor to every household in the area except theirs.

Joanna had found to her exasperation that to keep out of Cal Blackstone's way entirely was to risk social isolation. More and more she'd found herself running into him at point-to-points, parties and charity functions. To her annoyance, she'd actually been introduced to him a number of times by a series of well-meaning people who clearly shared Simon's view that it was time a truce was called in this family war.

But none of these people had been hounded and cheated by the Blackstones, Joanna thought violently. To them, Cal Blackstone was simply a charming young man, if a trifle sardonic, who drove a series of fast cars, dated all the most attractive girls in the West Riding, and could always be relied on for a hefty donation to any good cause. No one cared any more about past rights or wrongs, it seemed.

And once she and Cal Blackstone had been formally introduced, he took pains to remind her of the fact by seeking her out to greet her at every encounter. In fact, Joanna decided, he took an unpleasant delight in forcing himself on her notice, engaging her in conversation, and even inviting her to dance.

And the fact that she had ignored all his overtures and was never anything but icily civil in return seemed only to amuse him.

If she continued to keep him rigidly at a distance, eventually he would get tired of his cat-and-mouse games with her, she'd assured herself.

But she'd been wrong about that—totally wrong. Which was why she knew, none better, just what Cal Blackstone's real motives were, and exactly what he had planned for the remaining members of the Chalfont family.

She shivered, wrapping her arms defensively across her body, as she made herself relive once more in nerve-aching detail that rain-washed autumn afternoon on the high moor road above Northwaite when she'd discovered for herself how ruthless, how relentless an enemy he was ...

'Damnation!' Joanna stared down at the offside wheel of her Mini, her heart sinking. 'Of all times to get a flat tyre!' she muttered to herself, as she went to find the jack.

The rain was sweeping in sheets across the Northwaite valley below, and the hills were dankly shrouded in low cloud and mist.

By the time she'd fetched the jack, and squatted uncomfortably in the road beside the car, the rain had plastered her tawny blonde hair to her skull, and droplets of water were running down her forehead into her eyes, so that she had to pause every few seconds and brush them away.

She'd never had to change a tyre before, and she realised, to her shame, that she only had the haziest idea of how to go about it. Watching other people was not the same as personal experience, she decided wretchedly, as the jack stubbornly refused to co-operate with her efforts to fix it in place.

Send me someone to help this time, she bargained silently with her guardian angel, and I promise I'll sign on for a course in car maintenance this winter.

The thought had barely formed in her mind when the sleek grey Jaguar materialised silently out of the mist and slid to a halt behind her. She looked round eagerly, planning some self-deprecating, humorous remark about her predicament. Then the relieved smile died on her lips as she realised her rescuer's identity.

'Having trouble?' Cal Blackstone asked pleasantly, as he emerged from the driver's seat, shrugging on a waterproof jacket.

'I can manage, thanks,' Joanna said shortly. It occurred to her that her guardian angel must have a totally misplaced sense of humour.

'Then this must be a new method of wheel-changing of your own devising,' he said urbanely, folding his arms across his chest, and draping his tall, lean, elegant length against his own vehicle. 'How fascinating! I hope you'll allow me to watch.'

Apart from striking him down with a convenient boulder, or even the recalcitrant jack, Joanna could see no method of preventing him. Seething, she gritted her teeth and soldiered on. It was raining harder than ever now, and the damp was beginning to penetrate right through her layers of clothing to her skin, making her feel clammy and uncomfortable.

'You don't seem to be getting on very fast,' the hated voice commented at last.

'I don't like having an audience.'

'I can believe you don't like having me as an audience.' She wasn't looking at him, but there was something in his voice that told her he was grinning. 'Come on, Miss Chalfont, why don't you swallow your damned pride and say, "Help me"?'

'I didn't ask you to stop.'

'You wouldn't ask me to throw you a rope if you were drowning. As you probably will if this rain keeps up—that, or die of pneumonia.' He walked to her side, put his hand under her elbow and yanked her to her feet, without ceremony.

'Leave me alone!' She wrenched herself free of his grasp.

'Willingly—once this wheel of yours is changed.' He was fitting the jack into place with a deft competence that made her want to kill him and dance on his grave. 'Go and sit in my car, and dry yourself off a little,' he directed over his shoulder. 'If you look in the sports bag on the back seat, you'll find a towel.'

Instinct prompted her to reply haughtily that she preferred to remain where she was, but common sense intervened, reminding her that in this weather she would simply be cutting off her nose to spite her face, and that she was only laying herself open to further jibes.

The interior of the Jaguar smelt deliciously of leather upholstery mixed with a faint tang of some expensively masculine cologne.

Joanna sniffed delicately, grimacing a little as she extracted the towel from the bag, which was lying next to his squash racket on the rear seat. The towel, and the rest of the gear in the bag, was unused, so he must be on his way to the country club, but if so what was he doing on the high road, when there were other, more direct routes?

In spite of the towel's pristine condition, it was still his property, and she was deeply reluctant to use so personal an item. The idea of having to be beholden to him in any way affronted and revolted her. But she couldn't escape the fact that water was dripping dismally from her hair on to her face, and, after a brief internal tussle, she unfolded the towel and began to blot away the worst of the moisture.

With any luck, he would be the one to catch pneumonia, she thought, glaring through the windscreen at him as he worked. And, as if aware of her scrutiny Cal Blackstone looked round from his task, and waved.

With a snort of temper Joanna tossed the towel back into the bag and leaned back, savouring the undeniable comfort of her seat. Her father had driven a Jaguar when she was a small child, she remembered, and she'd always loved riding in it. She began to examine the dashboard and internal fittings, trying to remember what they'd been like in her father's day.

She'd been sitting with her father in the back of the Jaguar the first time she'd seen Cal Blackstone, she remembered with a shiver of pure distaste.

With regrettable promptitude, he appeared at the side of the car. 'Your wheel is duly changed, madam. Don't forget to have your damaged tyre mended.'

'I'm quite capable of working that out for myself,' she snapped.

'Of course.' He got into the driver's seat, and gave her a long look. His eyes were grey, she found herself noticing for the first time. Grey eyes, hard as steel, and cold as the skies above them. 'Please don't overwhelm me with gratitude.'

Joanna flushed at the sarcasm in his tone. 'Thank you,' she said stiffly. 'It was—fortunate that you were passing.'

'I often use this road,' he returned. 'I like the view of the Northwaite valley from up here.'

'If you can see it today, you must have X-ray vision.'

'I don't need to see it,' he said softly. 'I know what's there by heart. I've always known.' He pointed out into the mist and cloud. 'Away to your right is the country club. As you come down the valley, there are the chimneys of the Blackstone engineering works. They're generally what people notice first, just as my grandfather intended when he built the place. Then there's the Mill, relegated to second place these days, I'm afraid.' He paused for a moment as if expecting some response, some denial, and when there was none he continued, 'And finally, down to the left, well away from the pollution of the workers' houses in Northwaite, tucked away as if it's trying to hide, is Chalfont House.'

When he smiled, his teeth were very white. A predator's smile, Joanna thought, and her heart began to thump suddenly, harshly. 'Everything I own,' he said. 'And everything I intend to own before I've finished. Including you, Joanna Chalfont, you beautiful, hostile little bitch.'

For a moment she sat gaping at him, hardly able to credit what she'd just heard. Then,

'How dare you?' She could barely squeeze the words out of the frightening, painful tightness in her throat.

Cal Blackstone threw back his head and laughed. 'Said to the manner born,' he mocked. 'The well-born young lady rebuking the upstart pleb. It's wonderful what they teach you at those fancy Harrogate schools!'

'I think you must be insane,' said Joanna, fumbling for the handle of the door. 'I refuse to listen to any more of this.'

'You don't have to.' He was infuriatingly at his ease. 'I want you, and I'm going to have you. There's nothing more to be said.'

'Well, you couldn't be more wrong!' Joanna flung at him. She was trembling all over, fighting to keep her voice steady. 'I have a few things to say myself, and the first is that I wouldn't have you, Callum Blackstone, if you came gift-wrapped.'

He was still smiling. 'And what do you know about it?' he asked softly. 'What do you know about anything, Miss Chalfont, except pride and your own version of the past?' He shook his head slowly, his gaze locked with hers. 'It's time you began to think of the future, so let's start your thoughts in the right direction.'

The car door refused to budge under her frantic fingers. It was clearly linked to some central locking system outside her control, trapping her there alone with him.

Shrinking into the corner of her seat, Joanna saw Cal Blackstone reach for her, felt her shoulders grasped without gentleness, and her whole body drawn inexorably forward towards him. The smile had been wiped from his face, and his grey eyes glittered with something far removed from amusement. Something she barely understood, but, strangely, feared just the same.

She said, on a little sob, 'No—ah—no,' then his mouth was on hers and all further protest was stifled.

Nothing in her limited experience had prepared her for Cal's kiss and nothing could have done. He held her ruthlessly, crushing her soft breasts against the hard muscular wall of his chest, twining his hand in

her still-damp hair to hold her still, while his lips
plundered hers, relentlessly, hungrily—and endlessly.

She couldn't breathe. The scent of his skin filled
her nostrils with a sudden and desperate familiarity.
Tiny coloured lights danced frenetically behind her
closed lids. She felt physically overpowered, totally at
his mercy. She thought she might be going to faint,
and with the thought came a surge of anger, and con-
tempt for her own weakness.

He muttered against her lips, 'Open your mouth,'
and in a flash she saw her salvation. Pliantly she
obeyed. She felt his sigh of satisfaction, was aware
of his clasp slackening slightly so that he could turn
her in his arms, to hold her more easily against his
body, and as he relaxed she bit him hard, sinking her
teeth into his lower lip.

Cal jerked his head away, swearing, lifting a hand
almost unbelievingly to his bleeding mouth.

'You little shrew!'

'Try explaining that to your latest woman!' Joanna
flung at him. 'And, from now on, keep your distance
from me.'

He took a handkerchief from his pocket and dabbed
at the blood. To her fury he was grinning again.

'Not now I've had a taste of delights to come,
sweetheart.'

'You'll get nothing more from me as long as you
live! You might have been able to take advantage of
the situation today, but I'll make sure it never happens
again.'

'Ah, but it will,' he said softly. 'I may have lost the
first skirmish, Joanna, but the war's only just begin-

ning. And, I warn you, nothing but your complete surrender will do.'

She drew a swift, blazing breath, glaring at him. 'You're nothing but an animal, Cal Blackstone!'

He held out the bloodstained handkerchief, staring grimly back at her. 'Then I've certainly picked the right mate.'

'You've picked nothing and no one. From now on, keep out of my way!' She turned to wrestle with the door-handle, and to her chagrin it worked instantly.

'Our paths were made to cross.' His voice followed her as she stumbled out of the car. 'If you didn't know it before, you know it now. So drive carefully, my hot-tempered vixen. When I finally get to unwrap my gift, I want it to be perfect.'

She got to her car somehow, and sat, shaking, in the driving seat, waiting until the Jaguar slid past, and was swallowed up in the mist and rain.

She put up a cautious finger and touched the swollen contours of her mouth. Her lips felt bruised, but the greatest wound she'd suffered was humiliation.

She stared at the grey-soaked landscape, and thought, I'm afraid of him.

Now, in the drawing-room of Chalfont House, Joanna found the same words rising to her lips. *I'm afraid of him.*

She shook herself irritably. That was what came of letting herself remember—relive things best banished from her mind for good. But oh, God, it had been so real. She could swear she'd almost felt the pressure of Cal's mouth ravaging hers once more, tasted his blood...

Two years ago she had escaped him, but at what a price. She couldn't run away again. This time she had to stand her ground and fight him. She squared her shoulders, glancing up again at her grandfather's portrait.

'The war's on again, Grandpa,' she said. 'And this time I mean to win—for all our sakes.'

She had to. Because surrender on Cal Blackstone's terms was unthinkable.

CHAPTER TWO

THE mist swirled thickly above the high road. Joanna was lost in the depths of it, the damp tendrils wreathing about her, stifling her, confining her so that her limbs felt heavy and incapable of movement.

Yet she had to move—to run, because somewhere in the fog Cal Blackstone was waiting, his predator's hands reaching to stop her—to take her. She took one sluggish step, then another—and screamed aloud as a hand closed purposefully on her shoulder.

'Why, Miss Joanna, whatever's the matter with you?'

Perspiring, Joanna opened her eyes and found Nanny, comforting as the daylight pouring through the window, standing at her bedside with a cup of tea.

She managed a weak smile. 'Sorry, Nan, I must have been dreaming. Did I startle you?'

'It looks more as if you startled yourself, lass.' Nanny scrutinised her austerely. 'You're white as a sheet! Drink your tea while it's hot.'

A cup of tea, Joanna thought. Nanny's panacea for all ills from a headache to bereavement. She sat up, punching her tumbled pillows into shape. 'You're spoiling me.'

'Well, make the most of it. It won't happen so soon again,' Nanny said severely. 'And I've a message from Mr Simon.'

'...et me guess.' Joanna looked up at the ceiling. '...e's won a million pounds on the football pools and ...ll our problems are solved.'

Nanny snorted. 'Since when has Mr Simon done the pools?' she demanded. 'I'm to tell you that Mrs Chalfont was taken badly in the night, and he's gone with her to the nursing home.'

'You mean Fiona's started labour?' Joanna sat bolt upright. 'But the baby's not due for another couple of months. Oh, that's awful!'

'Don't waste your sympathy,' Nanny advised tartly. 'That baby won't be born until the right time, take my word for it. Madam's got indigestion, as I told her.' She snorted. 'What can she expect—sending Mr Simon into Northwaite at all hours for that tandoori chicken stuff?'

'Oh, is that all?' Joanna relaxed.

'Anyway, Mr Simon said to tell you if he's not back in time for the meeting this afternoon, you've to hold the fort. He said you'd understand.'

Joanna choked on a mouthful of tea. 'He said *what*?'

'You're not deaf. And don't spill that tea on your quilt.'

'But he can't do this,' Joanna said, half to herself. 'He's got to be back here in time—he's got to...' She looked up beseechingly at Nanny. 'The nursing home—they'll send Fiona home straight away if it's just indigestion, won't they?'

Nanny sniffed. 'The lord only knows. She might have discovered a few more symptoms by the time the doctor comes round. Madam's not averse to a few days in bed being waited on.'

Nanny could never be described as the you~
Chalfont's greatest fan, but Joanna had to adm.
spoke with a certain amount of justice. Once in
luxury of the nursing home, with attentive nurs
answering her every bell, Fiona might well be reluctant to return to Chalfont House where people were
more likely to tell her to pull herself together and stop
making a fuss about nothing. And she would certainly insist on Simon dancing attendance on her.

'After all,' Fiona had often pouted to him, 'it's your
fault I'm feeling so ghastly. It's your baby.'

Joanna groaned inwardly. Her plan to put several
miles between herself and Chalfont House prior to
Cal Blackstone's arrival was now plainly inoperable.

I could always ask him to postpone his visit, she
thought, but dismissed the idea almost as soon as it
had formed. The last thing she wanted, after all, was
Cal Blackstone to guess her deep reluctance to face
him. And at a wider, less personal level, any attempt
to put him off might be unwise at this juncture.

If Simon doesn't come back in time, I'll talk to him
myself, she decided grimly. And I'll let him know that
though he may have conned Si into thinking he's
Mister Nice Guy, he's got a fight on his hands with
me.

'Why, Miss Jo, you look really fierce. Whatever are
you thinking about?' queried Nanny.

'Getting up.' Joanna swallowed the rest of her tea,
and threw back the duvet. 'I think I'll have breakfast
with my father.' She paused. 'How is he today?'

'He's taking an interest in the cricket, according to
Gresham.' Nanny's face was expressionless. 'Reckons

should bring back Len Hutton as England ...n.'

Joanna sighed. 'Maybe they should at that.' She ...t a glance at the older woman. 'Nanny, we're ...aving a—visitor this afternoon, and I'd prefer if Dad knew nothing about it. I don't want him to be upset, especially if he's not—thinking too clearly.' She put on her robe and knotted the sash.

Nanny nodded. 'Gresham won't say owt, and I can stop Mrs Thursgood nattering. But am I to know who's expected?'

Joanna hesitated. 'It's Callum Blackstone.'

'A Blackstone crossing this doorstep?' Nanny gasped. 'I never thought I'd live to see the day!'

'Neither did I.' Joanna bit her lip. 'Believe me, Nanny, if I had a choice, I wouldn't let him within a mile of the place. But it's out of my hands.'

Nanny shook her head. 'Then you'll have to make the best of it, lass. Like the old saying, "Needs must when the devil drives."'

And that, Joanna thought wryly, as she made her way to the bathroom, seemed to sum the situation up with total accuracy.

Shrouded by the curtains at the long upstairs landing window, she watched him arrive. He was punctual, she noted without surprise. The Jaguar car he parked in front of the house—staking his claim at once, she thought bitterly—was the latest model. Nothing else had changed. He looked no older, no greyer, no heavier as he stood on the gravel below her, his gaze raking the blank windows as though he sensed her presence, and sought her.

Although she knew she couldn't be seen, Joanna felt herself shrink.

Oh, come on, she castigated herself. This is no way to start. After all, I know what he's planning, so there must be some way I can stop him.

But, for the life of her, she couldn't think of one.

As she heard the doorbell peal, she went on swift and silent feet back to her room, and waited for Mrs Thursgood to admit him.

She gave herself a long, critical look in the mirror. Her slim navy linen skirt, and the pure silk cream shirt she wore with it, looked neat and uncompromisingly businesslike. She'd drawn her hair severely back from her face and confined it at the nape of her neck with a wide navy ribbon.

She'd had plenty of time to prepare for this confrontation. Simon had phoned mid-morning to tell her that Fiona was being kept in for observation, at her own insistence.

'She's a bit fraught, Jo.' He'd sounded thoroughly miserable. 'Hit the roof when I suggested pushing off.' He'd paused. 'I feel an absolute worm about this. Do you think you can cope with Blackstone—feed him some story or other to keep him off for a while?'

'I can try,' she'd said wearily. 'Cheer up, Si. I hope Fiona feels better soon.'

Now Mrs Thursgood was tapping at her door. 'Your visitor's come, madam. I've put him in't drawing-room.'

Joanna counted to ten, breathing deeply, then walked sedately along the broad landing and down the stairs. She didn't hesitate at the drawing-room door, but went straight in, closing it behind her.

He was standing on the rug in front of the empty fireplace, studying her grandfather's portrait. At the sound of her entry, he turned, the grey eyes skimming over her, missing nothing.

'Good afternoon, Mrs Bentham.' The cool laconic voice grated on her. 'A historic moment, wouldn't you say?'

'Hardly a giant step for mankind, Mr Blackstone,' she returned with equal insouciance. 'Perhaps you'd like to state your business.'

'I'm sure your brother's informed you of the changes that have taken place during your—period of mourning.'

Joanna shrugged. 'I understand you now have a financial interest in the Craft Company.'

'It's more than that. As far as money's concerned, I am the Craft Company.' He glanced round. 'May I sit down?'

'If you wish.' She pretended faintly surprised amusement. 'Is this going to be a long interview? I do have other plans...'

'Then cancel them,' he said pleasantly, seating himself on the sofa. 'I'd prefer your undivided attention.' He leaned back, crossing his long legs. 'I gather Simon will not be joining us.'

She hesitated. 'His wife isn't very well.'

'I'm sorry to hear it.' He didn't sound even slightly regretful. 'She must take after her mother. She's thoroughly enjoyed very poor health for years. Apparently medical science is baffled.'

He'd captured the lady's martyred tones with wicked accuracy. To her annoyance, Joanna dis-

covered an unwilling giggle welling up inside
hastily turned it into a cough.

'Can we get back to the business in hand, pl
She took the armchair opposite to him. 'I sup
you want to know when you'll see some tangible retu
on your investment.'

'No,' he said. 'I'm prepared to bide my time on
that. There are other far more pressing matters between Simon and myself.' He reached into the inside
pocket of his jacket and extracted a small sheaf of
papers, held together by an elastic band. He tossed
them on to the low oak coffee-table between them.
'Do you know what these are?'

Her brows snapped together. 'How could I?'

'Then I suggest you take a look.'

Reluctantly she reached for the papers, and removed the band. As she studied them, her frown
deepened.

'I don't understand.'

'You're not a fool, Joanna,' he said quietly. 'You
know as well as I do that those are IOUs, and that
the signature on them is Simon's. They're gambling
debts that he ran up at the country club.'

Her mouth was dry suddenly. She'd been doing addition sums in her head as she riffled through them,
and the total she'd reached was horrifying, and still
incomplete.

She said, 'Gambling? But Si doesn't gamble.'

'He certainly doesn't gamble well. He's lost con-
sistently at poker, blackjack and roulette. He's exceeded the house limit for credit more than once as
well, and used my name to get more. I've had to bar
him from the gaming-rooms.' He saw the colour drain

face, and smiled sardonically. 'I presume
    ews to you.'

    said thickly, 'You know it is.'

    hen I may as well add that he's in hock to a bookie
Leeds for several thousand.'

She dropped the papers back on the table with an
expression of distaste. 'You're very well informed.'

'I find it pays to be.'

'Yet it's hardly ethical. Neither is your presence here
this afternoon. These—debts should be a private
matter between Simon and yourself, surely. You have
no right to involve me.'

'Sometimes private matters have a tiresome habit
of becoming incredibly public.' He seemed imper-
vious to the ice in her tone. 'And then you'd find
yourself involved right up to the hilt, my dear Mrs
Bentham. For instance, I could insist on having a spot
audit made at the Craft Company.'

The words hung in the air between them, challenging her.

She swallowed. 'And what would that prove, pray?'

'Perhaps nothing. But I'm afraid—I'm very much
afraid that there would be certain sums unaccounted
for. Simon had to find his stake money from somewhere, after all.'

'I don't believe you. In fact, I don't believe any of
this.' She flicked the IOUs with a contemptuous finger.
'If Simon had known you were going to raise any of
these matters this afternoon, he would have been here
in person. He thought you were coming to discuss the
Craft Company, and only that. Therefore he obviously has no guilty conscience...'

'A true Chalfont! Your grandfather had n~~~
science either. It's a pity Simon hasn't inherite~
strength as well.'

Joanna got to her feet. 'I think you'd better leave

'When I'm good and ready,' he retorted, making
no attempt to move. 'Sit down, Joanna, and hear me
out. Simon had good reason for failing to realise I
was about to call in his markers.'

She didn't want to hear any more. Her mind was
reeling, blanking out with sheer incredulity. Simon
gambling, she thought with horror. Losing thousands
he didn't possess and couldn't repay. What in the
world could possibly have started him on such a course
to disaster?

As if, she thought, I didn't know.

She lifted her head and stared at their enemy.
Steadying her voice, she asked, 'What good reason?'

'I promised I'd give him time, so he assumed he
was safe.'

'And what made you change your mind?'

'You did,' he said softly. 'You came home again,
Joanna. And that altered everything.'

'I fail to see why.' Her tone was defiant, but alarm
bells were sounding all over her nervous system.

He smiled at her. 'Oh, no, beauty, you haven't that
poor a memory. You put yourself temporarily out of
reach when you married Martin Bentham, but that's
all. And that's over. You knew it the day of the poor
bastard's funeral. Was that why you fled to the
States?'

She drew a sharp, painful breath. 'How dare you?'

'I dare quite easily,' he said. 'After all, I've waited
longer for you than for anything else in my life,

a, and, frankly, I'm beginning to run out of
nce.'

How unfortunate for you.' She invested her voice
th all the scorn she could muster. 'But I'm afraid
you're destined to go on waiting for a very long time.
For eternity, in fact.'

Cal shook his head. 'No, sweetheart. You're not
thinking clearly.' He pointed to the IOUs on the table
between them. 'As you so rightly said, these should
have remained a private matter between Simon and
myself. But in a war you use whatever weapons are
available, if you want to win. And I intend nothing
less than total victory.'

Joanna's hands clenched into fists. 'I'll see you in
hell——'

'And we'll both see your brother in the bankruptcy
court,' he interrupted harshly. 'I'll do it if I have to,
Joanna, and there isn't a soul in the world who would
blame me. He's behaved like a incompetent in his
business life, and a reckless fool privately. He should
be stopped sharply and permanently before he drags
himself, and everyone involved with him, any deeper
into the mire.'

He paused. 'On the other hand, the threat of it may
be enough to shock him to his senses, and impending
fatherhood may keep him there.'

'What do you care?' she asked bitterly. 'You helped
push him into this mess. You've used him and manipulated him all along the line for your own disgusting purposes...'

His mouth twisted. 'Have I? Then the more fool
Simon for letting me, wouldn't you say?'

'He's no match for you—he never was. He d
realise what he was getting into.'

Cal tutted. 'You mean you didn't try to warn him
How very remiss of you!'

'Of course I tried,' she said with angry weariness.
'But he wouldn't listen, and it was too late anyway.
He'd already handed the Craft Company to you on
a platter, the naïve, trusting idiot. He thought your
offer of help meant that the feud between us was over.'

'And so it will be soon,' he said softly. 'Every wrong
righted, every debt paid in full. The wheel come full
circle. A very satisfying state of affairs.'

'You're unbelievable!' Her voice shook. 'How can
these old quarrels still matter after all this time?'

He smiled. 'My grandfather always said revenge was
a dish best eaten cold.'

'I find that a nauseating idea.'

'Is that going to be your new refuge—self-
righteousness?' He sounded amused. 'It won't cut any
ice with me.'

'I'm sure it won't.' She put up a hand in a reveal-
ingly nervous gesture, and smoothed her hair back
over her ear. 'I suppose you're here to discuss your
terms. I can't say when Simon will be available——'

'He doesn't need to be.' The grey eyes glinted up
at her. 'As you're already well aware, the settlement
I have in mind involves just the two of us—you and
me. And I suggest, once again, that you sit down.'

She said thickly, 'I prefer to stand. Say what you
have to say, and go.'

He shrugged, and rose to his feet in one lithe, controlled movement. Like some jungle animal, she

...ght, flinching inwardly, flexing itself before the
...

'I told you my terms two years ago, Joanna. They
haven't changed. I want you.' He looked at her levelly.
'Come to me and I'll write off Simon's personal ob-
ligations to me, and his bookie friend.'

Joanna stood rigidly, feeling the colour drain out
of her face. It was like standing in the dock, she
thought dazedly, knowing you were innocent, but
hearing a life sentence pronounced just the same. She
wanted to scream aloud, to hit out in anger and re-
vulsion, but a small, cold inner voice warned her to
keep cool—keep talking—keep bargaining.

She lifted her chin. 'What about this house—our
home? Do you intend to take that too?'

'Originally, yes,' he said. 'But if you behave with
sufficient—er—generosity to me, I might be prepared
to match it, and leave it in Chalfont hands for your
father's lifetime at least.' He smiled at her sardonically. 'Its fate rests entirely with you, beauty.'

She bit her lip, her whole being cringing from the
implications in his words. 'And the Craft Company?
Will you leave that alone too?'

'I think you're beginning to overestimate the price
of your charms,' Cal Blackstone said drily. 'No, my
investment in the Craft Company stays—as insurance, if you like, for your continuing good
behaviour.'

Joanna closed her eyes for a moment. She said
evenly, 'I suppose there's no point in appealing to your
better nature. Reminding you that there are normal
standards of decency.'

'Tell me about it,' he said laconically. He gla
up at the portrait over the fireplace and his expres
hardened. 'At least I'm not evicting you witho
notice, throwing you on to the street.'

'And if I tell you that I do have standards—that I
have my pride and my self-respect? And that I'd rather
starve in the gutter than accept any part of your re-
volting terms?'

He shrugged again. 'Then that can be quite easily
arranged,' he returned. 'The choice is yours. But I
strongly advise you to think my offer over. You've
got twenty-four hours.'

'I don't need twenty-four seconds,' she said bitingly.
'You can do your worst, Mr Blackstone, and go to
hell!'

'I shall probably end there, Mrs Bentham,' he said
too courteously. 'But first I mean to order that independent audit I mentioned into the Craft
Company's accounts.' He paused. 'Simon may well
find himself facing more than a bankruptcy court.
How will the Chalfont pride cope with that, I
wonder?'

'I don't believe you. He wouldn't do such a thing.'
Her voice shook with the force of her conviction.

'Ask him,' he said. 'Some time during the next
twenty-four hours. Then call me with your final
answer.'

'You've had all the answer you're getting, you
bastard!' she said. 'I'll see you damned before I do
what you want!'

He gave her a sardonic look, as he retrieved the
papers from the coffee-table and slipped them back
into his pocket. 'Don't count on it, beauty. I promise

...hing—when you do call, I won't say that I told
so.'

Knuckles pressed to her mouth, Joanna stood like
statue as he made his way across the room to the
door. As it closed behind him, she bent and snatched
up a cut glass posy bowl, hurling it with all the force
of her arm at the solid panels.

'The swine!' she sobbed, as it shattered. 'Oh, God,
the unutterable bloody swine!'

She was like a cat on hot bricks for the rest of the
day waiting for Simon to return. It took all her self-
control not to drive over to the nursing home and
confront him there. She was sorely tempted, too, to
drive over to the Craft Company and do her own spot
check of the books.

But she discarded the idea. Such action would be
bound to provoke just the kind of comment she
wanted to avoid. And if, by the remotest chance, there
was something even slightly amiss ... She caught at
herself. That was the kind of poisonous reptile Cal
Blackstone was, she raged inwardly. Sowing discord
and distrust wherever he went.

She couldn't deny that Simon had been all kinds
of a fool, but she couldn't believe he was also a thief.
She wouldn't believe it.

'There's got to be some way out of this mess,' she
said aloud, through gritted teeth, as she paced the
length and breadth of the drawing-room. 'There's got
to be. Together we'll think of something. We have
to!'

She swallowed convulsively as that same small voice
in her head reminded her of the sheer magnitude of

what was threatening them all. The loss of their ⎯
the destruction of their remaining business ven⎯
and personal disgrace for Simon—and all at the wo⎯
possible time, if there was ever a good time for suc⎯
things to happen, she acknowledged wryly.

It was no good telling herself that it was all Simon's
own fault, and he'd have to find some remedy himself.
She couldn't leave him to sink if she could help him
to swim. But she couldn't sacrifice herself either.

Cal Blackstone's words rang like hammer blows
inside her brain. 'I want you. Come to me...'

He's just offered me the ultimate insult, she told
herself, by presuming I'd even consider such a degrading suggestion. He's misjudged me completely.

Yet he'd summed up some of her past reactions with
disturbing accuracy, she recalled unwillingly. His
comments about her marriage to Martin had been too
close to the mark for comfort.

She shivered. What was she saying? She'd loved
Martin, of course she had. He'd been sweet and safe
and *there*, and she'd thought that was enough. She'd
convinced herself that it was.

Only it wasn't, she thought wretchedly. How could
it be? And it was disaster for both of us.

On the day of his funeral, she'd stood in the small
bleak churchyard in the conventional black dress of
the widow, feeling drained of emotion, totally ob-
jective, as if all this tragedy were happening to some
other person. She could even remember being thankful
that the demure veiling on her equally conventional
hat concealed the fact that she was completely tearless.

Then she'd looked up and seen Cal Blackstone
staring at her. He'd been standing on the edge of the

rowd of mourners, but his head wasn't bent in
or common respect. There had been bitterness
he look he sent her, and condemnation, and over-
ing all a kind of grim triumph.

Don't think I've given up, his glance had told her.
This marriage of yours was just an obstacle which has
now been removed. And now I'm coming after you
again.

The knowledge of it had been like a blow, knocking
all the breath out of her body. Involuntarily, instinctively, she'd taken a step backwards in instant negation, her foot stumbling on a tussock of earth.

'Be careful, my dear!' Her father had insisted on
attending the ceremony with her, standing bareheaded at her side in the windswept graveyard, and
she'd snatched at his arm for comfort and support as
she'd done when she was a small girl, and a crowd of
jeering boys had thrown earth and stones at their car.

Oh, I will, she'd promised herself silently. I'll take
more care than I've ever done in my whole life.

Aunt Vinnie's letter offering her sanctuary had
been, like Martin's proposal of marriage, a godsend,
a lifeline, and she'd snatched at that too, telling herself that Cal Blackstone would eventually resign himself to the fact that she was gone, and abandon his
crazy obsession about her.

He wasn't really serious about it, she'd assured
herself over and over again. For heaven's sake, he was
never short of female companionship, so he wasn't
exactly single-minded about his pursuit of her, if she
could call it that. He didn't chase her, yet he always
seemed to be there, like a dark shadow on the edge

of her world, a winter storm threatening the brightness of her horizon.

If she went away, and stayed away, with luck he'd forget her, and get safely married to one of the many willing ladies he escorted. Time and distance would solve everything. That was what she'd thought. That was how she'd reassured herself.

But how wrong was it possible to be? Joanna thought broodingly, as she paced restlessly up and down. Cal Blackstone hadn't just been making mischief and trying to alarm her, as she'd secretly hoped and prayed. He'd meant every word, and that warning look he'd sent her at Martin's funeral had been nothing less than a stark declaration of intent.

And typical of his appallingly tasteless behaviour, she thought with a fastidious shudder, then paused, a hysterical bubble of laughter welling up inside her.

Why the hell was she worrying about something as trivial as the way he'd treated her as a widow in mourning, when he was now threatening her and her entire family with total humiliation and ruin?

While she'd thought herself safe in the States, Cal Blackstone had been busy ensnaring Simon in a web of financial dependency, both personal and professional. Then he'd sat back and waited, like the spider, for the unsuspecting fly to return...

But that was defeatist talk, she told herself in self-reproach. After all, if the fly struggled hard enough, even the strongest web could be broken.

She was halfway through a dinner she had no interest in eating when Simon eventually came in. He looked tired and anxious, and for a moment she was tempted to leave him in the peace he so clearly needed at least until the morning.

She let him talk for a while about Fiona and the labour pains which had so unaccountably subsided while he ate his meal.

Then she said quietly, 'Don't you want to know what happened this afternoon?'

He shrugged, his face adopting a faintly martyred expression. 'I suppose so. To be honest, Jo, although his letter threw me when it arrived, I've been thinking about it while I've been hanging around at the nursing home, and, frankly, I don't know what all the fuss is about. Things at work are picking up slowly. He'll get his money back, and he'll just have to be patient, that's all. I hope you told him so.'

She picked up the coffee-pot and filled two cups with infinite care.

'I didn't actually get the chance,' she said. 'He didn't come here to talk about work. It was your other debts he was concerned with. The ones you ran up at the casino, and the race-track.'

She watched him go white. There was a long, painful silence. Then he said very rapidly, 'He told you that, but he had no right. He said there was no hurry. He knew I'd pay it all off if he just gave me time.'

'How?' She looked at Simon's guilty, miserable face and knew that the question was unanswerable.

She nerved herself to go on. 'He—he did mention the Craft Company in one context. He talked about the books—the accounts.'

'What about them?' Simon's gaze was fixed on the polished dining table.

'He said something about an independent audit,' Joanna said, and stopped appalled as Simon's cup dropped from his hand, spilling coffee everywhere.

'Can he do that?' The blue eyes were scared, imploring. 'Can he, Jo?'

'Is there some reason why he shouldn't?' She tried to speak evenly, but her voice trembled as she realised she had to face, to come to terms with the unthinkable.

He didn't reply, just picked up his table napkin and began blotting up the coffee as if it were the most important thing in the world.

She said, 'It's true, then. There's money missing, and you're responsible.'

'Whose bloody company is it anyway?' he said, his tone mutinous, defensive.

'Not yours to that extent. Simon, are you crazy?'

'I had to do something. Fiona was miserable, and needed a break. She had her heart set on St Lucia. She's never known what it is to be short of cash—she doesn't understand.'

Joanna closed her eyes for a moment, trying to visualise Fiona's reaction to the news that her husband had made them bankrupt and homeless. But her imagination balked at the very idea.

'Go on,' she said, with infinite weariness. 'So you embezzled money from the Craft Company to take Fiona on an expensive holiday.'

'I did not embezzle it!' Simon's face was flushed now with anger. 'I borrowed it.'

'With Philip's knowledge and permission?'

'I didn't think it was necessary to mention it to him. After all, it was only a couple of thousand or so on emporary loan. I fully intended to pay it back. One damned good win at blackjack was all I needed.'

'But you didn't win.'

'No, I started losing really badly. I kept telling myself my luck would change, but it didn't. It just kept getting worse.'

'Then why on earth didn't you stop?'

'I couldn't,' he said simply. 'I had to go on trying to win.'

Joanna ran the tip of her tongue round her dry lips. 'Did you borrow any more money?' she asked carefully.

'Some,' he muttered. 'I'd have been all right—I know I would—if bloody Blackstone hadn't barred me from the casino. How the hell was I supposed to recoup my losses if I wasn't allowed to play?' He gave her a petulant look. 'I still don't see why he found it necessary to drag you into all this. I thought we had a gentlemen's agreement about it.'

'Cal Blackstone,' she said quietly, 'is no gentleman. Tell me, Si, and I want the truth—is there any hope that you'll be able to repay at least the—loan from the firm?'

There was a pause, then he shook his head. 'I can't. Philip and I are both drawing minimum salaries at the moment. And I've had so much extra expense with the baby coming. The nursing home fees cost a fortune for a start.' His expression became alarmed. 'Blackstone won't really insist on this audit, will he? I mean—I can explain to old Phil, and I'm sure he'd understand, but I'd rather not.'

Joanna murmured something non-committal, but in her heart she wasn't at all convinced that old Phil would be quite so amenable to the news that some of their slender profits had been illegally squandered on gambling, and vacations in the West Indies.

'So what does Blackstone want?' Simon demanded apprehensively.

Joanna hesitated. 'I'm not altogether sure,' she prevaricated. 'Now that I know his—allegations are true, I have to get back to him—work something out.'

'Oh, goody.' Simon's voice was heavily sarcastic. 'I didn't realise that you two were so much in each other's confidence. Yesterday you couldn't stand the sound of his name. Today you've got your heads together, deciding what to do for the best about poor misguided Simon. Does he get his knuckles rapped, or just stand in the corner?'

Joanna bit her lip. 'That kind of attitude doesn't help.'

'And having my private affairs chewed over behind my back isn't totally acceptable either,' Simon retorted furiously. 'You should have refused to listen—referred him straight to me, instead of meddling in what doesn't concern you.'

Joanna held on to her temper with an effort. 'If you're charged with embezzlement, it will concern me very closely,' she said evenly. 'It will concern us all. And imagine the effect it could have on Daddy.'

'Oh, yes, let's.' Simon's face was stony. 'Look, everyone, Simon's been a naughty boy. And Joanna's the blue-eyed girl who's going to put everything right. Well, bloody good luck to you!' He glared at her. 'What a pity you didn't stay here and pitch in after Martin died, instead of swanning off to the States. Things might have been different then.' He scraped

...s chair back and rose. 'I'm going back to the nursing
home to stay with Fiona. Have your high-level con-
ference with Blackstone, sister dear, and get everything sorted. Feel free to let me know some time what's
been decided for me.'

He went out, banging the door behind him, and
seconds later she heard the front door slam too, and
his car start up and drive away.

Joanna leaned back in her chair, trembling a little.
She knew Simon of old. Once offended, he would
sulk unreasonably for days, and she wouldn't be able
to get a sensible word out of him.

He would come round eventually, she thought, but
she didn't have that kind of time. All she had was
twenty-four hours, and they were fast running out.

Even after Martin's accident, she had never felt so
helpless, so alone—so vulnerable.

She thought, What am I going to do? And, fiercely,
What can I do?

But she knew the answer to that, only too well.
Everything she held dear in this world was in danger,
and she, uniquely, held the key to its salvation.

This, she thought, is how an animal must feel when
the trap closes round it.

She sat for a long time, gazing, with dead eyes, into
space. Then, her mind made up, she went into the
hall, lifted the telephone receiver, and began, slowly,
to dial.

CHAPTER THREE

DOWN by the reservoir, there was a breeze blowing off the water. Joanna lifted her face to it gratefully as she strolled along the path towards the dam. The car journey had seemed stifling, but that might have been because she was so nervous.

She took a deep breath, then stood for a moment, watching the manoeuvres of the solitary sailing dinghy using the sparkling expanse of water. At the weekends, the water was alive with multi-coloured sails, but on a mid-week afternoon privacy was almost guaranteed.

She glanced edgily at her watch. She'd arrived early, and there was still a short while to go before their meeting.

Cal Blackstone had raised no objection, the previous evening, when she had haltingly suggested the reservoir as a rendezvous. She couldn't explain even now why she'd felt so desperate to face him on neutral territory, in the open air, away from the confines of Chalfont House.

She'd tried to work out in advance what she was going to say. In fact she'd spent an entire sleepless night trying and discarding various approaches to the subject. But nothing seemed right.

But then how could it? Joanna could almost believe, even now, that this was simply a particularly vivid nightmare from which she would soon thankfully waken. Maybe she should just raise her hands surrender and say, 'You win,' she thought, ımacing.

She retied the sleeves of the turquoise sweater she was wearing slung across her shoulders more securely, and resumed her walk.

She'd spent the morning with her father, who was having what Gresham called 'one of his far-off days'. He'd been sitting in his wheelchair beside the open window, with an old photograph album on his knees, slowly turning the pages as if they held the answer to some mystery he was desperate to solve. Joanna had sat beside him, trying to take an interest in the faded prints. After all, these picnics, carriage outings and stiltedly posed groups constituted a large part of the Chalfont family history, she'd thought, so it was a pity there were so many missing, and that so few of the others had been captioned with names. Her grandfather was instantly recognisable, of course, and she'd supposed the rather downtrodden woman beside him in some of the photos was her grandmother, but when she'd mentioned this to her father he'd stared at her vaguely, and said, 'Joanna. That was her name—Joanna.'

And as she'd been named after her, that was something his daughter knew already.

She'd looked wistfully around the room, filled with her father's favourite pieces of furniture. His desk from the study, a high-backed armchair beside the fireplace, the pipe rack Simon had made for him at school, they were all there. Anything that might help him retain his precarious hold on reality. The walls were hung with his best-loved paintings too, and his collection of books was stored in a revolving bookcase close to his chair.

Not that he read much these days, she thought, stifling a sigh. His concentration span was too erratic for that. Gresham read to him, mostly from the newspapers, and Joanna had also taken part since her return, using mainly short pieces from anthologies, and poems that she knew he liked. Sometimes he seemed to remember, but most of the time he didn't. She wondered sadly if he would forget her too once she no longer lived at Chalfont House.

'Planning to throw yourself in, Joanna?'

She started violently. She'd been so deep in her reverie, she hadn't been aware of Cal Blackstone's approach, until he was standing right beside her.

'I'm not the suicidal type,' she said, recovering herself swiftly. 'But I might make a good murderess.'

'That explains your choice of meeting-place, no doubt.' He looked around him with appreciation. 'Perhaps I should warn you that I'm a strong swimmer.' He perched on the guard-rail separating the path from the water, and looked at her. She returned his gaze unwillingly. He was casually dressed today in cream trousers that hugged his strong thighs and long, muscular legs, and a short-sleeved navy shirt, open at the neck. His chest and forearms were tanned, and shadowed with dark hair. She was sharply and disturbingly aware of his strong male physicality. Hurriedly she looked past him to the water.

'And also there's a witness.' She pointed to the dinghy and its occupant.

'So it will have to be ground glass in my porridge after all.'

She winced inwardly at this passing reference to the fact that they would soon be having breakfast together. God, but he was sure of himself, she thought bitterly.

'I presume you've talked to Simon,' Cal went on.

'Yes.' She paused. 'It seems you were right. But it won't be necessary to do an audit. I've decided to make up the deficit myself with some money I—happen to have.'

'He doesn't deserve that.'

'He's my brother,' Joanna said shortly. She gave him a straight look. 'Now that I'm back in Northwaite for good, I'm planning to get work of some kind. I want to know if you'll allow me to pay off his gambling debts out of my salary as and when I can afford it.'

'You'd actually be prepared to do that?'

'Yes, I would,' she said. 'Simon's weak, and he's been a fool—I acknowledge that. But if you go ahead with your threat and make him bankrupt, then Fiona will leave him, and, although I don't care for her very much, he'll have lost everything in the world that he loves.'

'My offer stands,' he said softly. 'It is not open to negotiation. But then you knew that already, didn't you?'

'I hoped,' she said, 'that some last-minute stirrings of decency might prevail with you.'

'I've always found them an unnecessary luxury,' he said calmly. 'Stop beating about the bush, Joanna. Do you accept my offer or not?'

In the folds of her cream dress, her hands were balled into fists, the nails scoring the soft flesh of her palms. She looked past him at the encircling hills, patterned by sunlight and cloud.

'I must,' she said. 'I won't let your sick plans wreck Simon's marriage.'

'He'd probably be better off without the silly bitch.'

'Or lose him his unborn child.'

Cal Blackstone's smile was satirical. 'A boy to carry on the Chalfont name?'

'Perhaps.'

'How very dynastic.'

'Isn't that what all men want?'

He shrugged. 'I'm unable to speak for the world at large. For myself, I have no immediate plans to make you pregnant, if that's what you want to know.'

Joanna was aware of a ridiculous urge to blush. 'I'm pleased to hear it.' She made her voice as offhand as possible. 'For the record, what are your immediate plans?'

He looked meditatively down at the water. 'I thought we might have dinner together this evening.' He paused. 'Followed, of course, by breakfast tomorrow morning.'

It was no more than she'd expected, and exactly what she'd feared.

Dry-throated, she said, 'You—don't waste any time, do you?'

'I've wasted far too much already.' He looked her over, brows raised. 'Don't look so stricken, Mrs Bentham. You've been married, and survived. You know what happens.'

She made herself stare back at him. 'Is that a proposal, Mr Blackstone?'

He grinned. 'Not at all. I'm not the marrying kind.'

'And how long is this—informal arrangement destined to last?' she asked with icy scorn.

'Until I decide to call a halt.' His eyes lingered on the thrust of her breasts under her thin dress, as intimately as a caress. 'Don't hope for any miracles.'

'I hope for nothing from you.'

His smile widened insolently. 'Now that's carrying pessimism too far.' He paused, watching the colour flood into her face. 'I shall expect you to join me at the country club at eight this evening,' he went on. 'And don't make me come and fetch you, because that would annoy me.'

'I'm shivering in my shoes,' she flung at him, furious with herself for blushing.

'No, lass, not you.' He swung himself off the rail, dusting off his trousers. 'You're not a weakling like Simon. You're a chip off the old block. Taming you, Joanna Chalfont, is going to be a privilege as well as a pleasure.'

'You're disgusting, Callum Blackstone!' She held herself very straight. 'I loathe and despise you, and I always will!'

He laughed, running a hatefully casual finger down the curve of her warm cheek. 'Tell me that again in the morning,' he said, and walked away from her up the path towards the car park.

Joanna was suddenly aware that her breathing was as hurried as if she'd been taking part in some marathon race, and that her legs had turned to jelly, but she made herself stand there, unmoving and defiant, until his car started up, and turned on to the road above.

She saw him lower the window and lean out, lifting his hand in a mocking salute.

'Until tonight.' The words came to her faintly, and were instantly picked up by the crowding hills, and echoed back with disagreeable triumph, and all too distinctly. Until tonight—until tonight...

With a little sob, Joanna pressed her hands over her ears, and began to stumble up the path towards her own vehicle.

Damn him, she thought violently. Damn him for all eternity!

Joanna's watch said eight o'clock precisely as she walked up the steps and through the revolving door into the foyer of the country club.

The dark, pretty receptionist gave her a welcoming smile. 'Can I help you, madam?'

I wish you could, Joanna thought. Aloud, she said, 'Mr Blackstone is expecting me.'

The girl discreetly consulted a clipboard under the broad mahogany desk. 'Oh, yes, Mrs Bentham. If you'd like to leave your wrap, Gregory our head waiter will take you to Mr Blackstone's table in the restaurant. Mr Blackstone is waiting for a telephone call from the States, and will join you as soon as possible.'

Joanna surrendered the fringed embroidered shawl she was wearing over her black dress, and followed a deferential Gregory through a luxuriously fitted cocktail bar to the dining-room beyond. It was an elegant room, its lavishly decorated ceiling supported by gilded pillars, and with french windows running the length of one wall. Although it was still relatively early, more than half the tables were already occupied, many of them by people Joanna knew, she realised with embarrassment. She was aware of a battery of interested glances as Gregory conducted her with some ceremony to a table set for two and discreetly placed in a corner of the room, which in turn was half screened by a trellis of climbing plants.

The first thing she saw was the bottle of champagne waiting on ice. The second was the perfect crimson rose just beginning to unfurl its petals in the centre of the table. Her lips tightened angrily.

'May I get you a drink, madam?' Gregory asked as he seated her.

'Perrier water, please, with a twist of lemon.'

She was glad that the table was comparatively private, but knew that the damage had already been done, and quite deliberately too. Everyone in the restaurant would know that this was the first time she'd ever set foot in the country club, just as Cal Blackstone intended. They would also know this was his private table she was sitting at, and be putting two and two together to arrive at some amazing totals. The gossip and rumour would spread out from the Northwaite valley like the ripples from a stone dropped into a pool of water, she thought contemptuously.

What none of them would actually guess was the truth. Because that defied belief.

Her drink arrived and she sipped it, glaring at the champagne and the rose. How dared he? How dared he treat this as if it were some kind of love tryst, a cause for celebration, instead of the vile, sordid assignation that it really was?

She wished she had the guts to cause another sensation by throwing the whole shooting match through the nearest window and then marching out. But she knew that Cal Blackstone would be totally unamused by such behaviour, and that any retribution would be visited on Simon, not on herself. I can't risk that, she thought.

She'd hoped to see Simon when he came home from work, but he'd eaten an early dinner and departed for the nursing home while she was upstairs dressing. Clearly he was still in a profound huff.

She had left a message with Gresham that she was going to be out overnight, staying at a friend's, and no one was to worry, then fled to her car before Nanny could find her and start putting her through the usual inquisition. If she lied, Nanny would know at once. Yet how could she tell her the truth? In Nanny's book, unwed people courted in a respectable manner, and did not share a roof, let alone a bed, before the wedding ceremony, even in the nineteen nineties. Joanna's fall from grace would be roundly and endlessly condemned.

She sighed inwardly. At best, she was only postponing a series of awkward confrontations which would become inevitable when talk got back to Chalfont House. She would obviously have Simon to explain to as well. And no doubt Fiona and her ghastly mother would have their say in addition.

There was a sudden stir in the restaurant, and with a sinking heart she knew that Cal was on his way. Her fingers tightened achingly around the tumbler.

'Darling, can you forgive me? My call from the States was delayed.'

She looked up, saw Gregory hovering attentively at his shoulder and forced a poor imitation of a smile. 'It doesn't matter. I've been well looked after.'

'You must be starving.' Cal sat down, signalling for menus to be brought. 'What would you like to eat?'

The beautiful copperplate handwriting seemed to dance meaninglessly before her eyes. Her throat was closing up suddenly, and she was trembling all over. She put the menu down.

'I can't go through with this,' she said hoarsely.

'Come now, beauty, my chef isn't that bad.'

'This is not a joke.' She pounded a desperate fist on the immaculate tablecloth. 'It is not funny!'

'No,' he said. He was still smiling, but his eyes were like chips of ice. 'It isn't. We have a bargain, Mrs Bentham, and by God you're going to keep your side of it. Or does Brother Simon's welfare no longer seem so important to you?'

'You know it does. But there must be some other way. You—you can't want me like this—hating you.'

'You spent six months of your life sleeping with a man you didn't give a damn about.' Cal shrugged a shoulder. 'At least hatred implies passion—of a sort. I prefer that to indifference.'

'How dare you?' Joanna's violet eyes flared. 'You know nothing about my relationship with Martin. You're not fit to mention his name!'

'Don't be silly,' he said wearily. 'I was at school with him. And you and I both know perfectly well why you married him as you did. They say "Marry in haste, repent at leisure", don't they? Well, you've done your penance, Joanna. Now you can start to live again.'

'With you?' she threw at him bitterly.

'With no one else,' he said. 'And you'd better believe that.'

'If you take me, it will be rape.'

He studied her flushed, pleading face for a long moment, his firm lips smiling faintly.

'No,' he said at last, 'it won't. I promise you that, Joanna.'

'What else can it be, when the very thought of you nauseates me?'

'Then stop thinking,' he said. 'Have something to eat instead, and you'll start to feel better. I can recommend the Dover sole.'

'It would choke me.'

'I wouldn't blame it,' he said drily. He put his menu down. 'Go hungry, then, if you feel you're making some valid moral point. I intend to have clear soup, and the fillet steak, rare. I'm sure you can make some capital out of that.'

When Gregory came for their order, Joanna said curtly that she would have melon and Dover sole. She didn't look at Cal, but the expected sarcastic comment did not come.

She watched in hostile silence as the champagne was opened.

When the wine waiter departed, she said coldly, 'Is there supposed to be something to celebrate?'

'That might be pushing it, I agree,' he said, his mouth twisting. 'Although we could always drink to the final burying of the hatchet between us.' He gave her inimical expression a quizzical glance. 'No? Then let's regard this more in the nature of a launch, a beginning.' He lifted his glass in a toast. 'To our better understanding, Joanna. We'll leave it at that.'

She hesitated, then took a reluctant sip.

'Bravo,' he said silkily. 'I know what that must have cost you.'

The meal when it came was excellent. Cal chatted easily on purely non-personal topics while they ate, or while Joanna pushed her food round the plate in a pretence of eating, and returned monosyllabic responses when required. How could he behave so normally, she wondered, seething, as if this were just any social occasion?

'Would you like some dessert?' he asked as the table was cleared.

She shook her head. 'Just coffee, please.'

'Then we'll have that upstairs,' he said. 'I make very good coffee.'

It was too late to do an about-face and demand the sweet trolley. Joanna crumpled her napkin and got slowly to her feet.

There was a lift, marked 'Private'. He ushered her into it, and pressed the button. She leaned against the metal wall, feeling her heart fluttering against her ribcage, as the lift rose all too swiftly. The palms of her hands felt clammy, but he might notice if she tried to wipe them on her skirt.

The lift stopped and the doors slid open. She emerged and walked across a carpeted passage to an imposing pair of double doors. He unlocked them and stood aside to allow her to precede him into the room.

It was huge, with tall Georgian windows looking towards the western evening sky. The heavy cream brocade curtains were undrawn, to admit the last vestiges of daylight, but the lamps had been lit and glowed softly on tables and in alcoves. The furnishings, she saw, were comfortable without being ostentatious, and traditional in concept rather than trendy. It was neither vulgar nor *nouveau riche*, as she'd half expected, and she didn't know whether to be glad or sorry.

'Sit down.' Cal gestured towards one of the deeply cushioned sofas. 'And I'll see to the coffee.' He pointed to a door. 'That's the kitchen.' He paused. 'And the bedroom and bathroom are over there.'

Joanna deliberately avoided looking in the direction indicated. 'Everything opens out of this room?' she asked stiltedly.

He nodded. 'I had the whole of the first floor of this wing remodelled, and simplified. When I'm at home and relaxing, I don't want to have to walk down a lot of unnecessary passages to reach what I need.'

Joanna had too often bewailed the Victorian inconveniences of Chalfont House to argue with that.

She sat rigidly on the edge of the sofa, listening to him moving around the kitchen, the chink of crockery, the sound of a percolator. The aroma of coffee drifted persuasively into the room.

In the deepening velvet sky beyond the windows, stars were beginning to appear, and she could hear music, slow and dreamy, emanating from some other part of the building.

She was surrounded by all the elements of a romantic idyll, she thought helplessly, yet in reality she was being subjected to the crudest form of blackmail. He couldn't really mean it, she told herself. He was stringing her along, playing a cruel joke. He had to be. Didn't he?

'Revenge,' he'd said. 'A dish best eaten cold.' No joke in that, she thought, and a long aching shiver ran through her.

He returned with the tray, which he set down on a table in front of the sofa.

'Cream and sugar?' he asked.

'Just cream, please,' said Joanna, staring down at the carpet. She accepted the cup he handed her, and swallowed some of the strong, powerful brew. It seemed to put heart into her—to give her the courage to make one last appeal to him.

She put the cup down, and said, 'Tell me something—why are you doing this?'

For a moment he said nothing, and she went on hurriedly, 'I mean, you don't need to—to force women to be with you. So why me?'

'Because you've been a thorn in my flesh for too long and for too many reasons,' he said quietly. 'And because I know that I wouldn't have got within a mile of you in any other way.' He smiled with a kind of reminiscent bitterness. 'Every time I met you socially, you used to look at me as if I were the worst kind of dirt. You seemed to be encased in ice, always at a distance, even when you were a little girl. You were either away at school, or shut up in that big barracks of a house.' He paused, his mouth twisting slightly. 'Or riding round in your father's car like a little princess.'

'I remember that well,' she said savagely. 'I remember those yobs throwing stones at us, while you egged them on.'

She'd been so frightened. She'd cowered in the back seat beside her father, holding his arm, listening to the jeering and catcalls and the thudding of missiles against the side of the car.

'Who are they, Daddy?' she'd wailed.

'They're local scum, my pet, not worth your notice,' Anthony Chalfont had said scornfully. 'Sit up, Joanna, and show them you're not afraid. Harris, hurry up and get us out of here.'

She'd been scared half to death, but she'd obeyed him, lifting her chin and staring disdainfully at the gang of youths at the side of the road. It was then she'd seen him.

He was taller than any of the others, and standing a little way apart. He was wearing the same anonymous jeans and sweater, yet there was something about him that told her that he was different. That he was the leader, and always would be.

He was smiling, openly enjoying their discomfiture, as the chauffeur, cursing under his breath, edged the big car along the narrow street. He saw Joanna and laughed out loud, pointing at her, and calling out something to the others.

Thick mud splattered the window beside her, and Joanna cried out and jerked away.

'It's all right, sweetie,' her father said gently, as the car gathered speed out of Northwaite. 'They've gone.'

'They're vile!' she said passionately, looking at the mud dripping down the window. 'They've spoiled our car. And that big boy was the worst. He was laughing, making them do it. Who was he?'

Her father's mouth compressed. 'I've no idea, Joanna,' he said repressively. 'I can't be expected to know the identity of louts from the slums.'

Some instinct told her that he was not telling her the whole truth, but now was not the time to pursue it. Instead, she bearded Harris while he was cleaning the motor which was his pride and joy.

'Is the car going to be all right, Harris?'

'Reckon it will, Miss Jo. No great harm done.'

'That's good.' She stood watching him polishing the chrome. 'Why did they do it, do you suppose? We didn't even know them.'

Harris shrugged. 'Times are hard just now, Miss Jo, and tempers run high sometimes.'

'Oh.' Joanna wasn't sure what he meant, but there was something more important she wanted to ask. 'Harris—that boy—the one who was making the others throw stones at us. Who was he? My father said he didn't know.'

'Happen he didn't recognise him, Miss Jo,' Harris said laconically. 'He's been away to school and grown a fair bit since your father last laid eyes on him.' He snorted. 'That was Cal Blackstone, that was.'

Now, nearly fifteen years on, Cal Blackstone said frowningly, 'If you're going to remember things like that, remember them right. They weren't throwing stones, you little idiot, just clods of earth, and the odd empty can.'

'But you were encouraging that pack of hooligans in their disgusting behaviour. Getting them to throw things at us just because our name was Chalfont.'

'Is that what your father told you?' His mouth tautened contemptuously. 'Well, it figures. Let me make one thing plain, Joanna—any mud-slinging going on wasn't my idea. Although I will admit I did nothing to stop it until I saw how scared you were,' he added.

'You were directing operations—laughing at us!'

'My God,' he said slowly, staring at her, 'it did make an impression on you. Yes, I laughed. I enjoyed seeing the lordly Mr Chalfont on the receiving end of some dirt for once. Do you know who those lads were, by any chance? Did Daddy tell you they were the sons of some of the men he'd just laid off from his mill without warning? I bet he didn't.' His voice hardened. 'They'd all lived with unemployment before, and they were—reacting accordingly. You wouldn't understand anything about that, would you, Joanna? Your family may not be lords of the Northwaite valley any more, but you've never had to stand in the queue for free school meals, or wear jumble sale clothes. Or pray that the giro comes on time.'

Her face flamed. 'Don't you dare criticise my father! He did his best to keep the mill going—to provide work. Men were laid off in other places as well.'

He shrugged. 'But he couldn't understand that times were changing, or change with them. In the woollen industry, only the strong and adaptable survive. But I don't blame him entirely. Your grandfather's interpretation of strength was pig-headedness and bullying, so by the time your father took over it was too late.'

'You don't need to make excuses for him or any member of my family,' she said bitingly.

'I'd find it hard in Simon's case, certainly.'

'You have the arrogance—the unmitigated gall to say that? Simon wouldn't be in all this financial mess if it weren't for you. You led him into it deliberately!'

He stared at her incredulously for a moment, then burst out laughing. 'Now I've heard everything! Let me tell you something, beauty. Where temptation's concerned, your brother needs no leading. I first barred him from using the casino several years ago because I could see he was going to be trouble, and I had the feeling I would be blamed for it somehow. Nor did I take him by the hand and introduce him to his bookmaker either. He managed that all by himself.'

He shook his head. 'No, Joanna, if you think Simon's problems are down to some deep Machiavellian plotting by me in order to get my hands on your delectable body, then you flatter yourself. The circumstances were there, and I decided to turn them to my advantage, that's all.'

'All?' she said chokingly. 'My God—all!'

'What was I supposed to do? Ring you and ask for a date? You'd have hung up on me. Send you flowers? They'd have gone straight in the bin. Come calling on you to the house? You'd have told whatever servants you have left to throw me out.'

'You had another choice. You could have left me alone.'

'I tried that, beauty, while you were married, and when you ran away to America. It didn't work.' He poured out some more coffee and handed her cup to her. 'Now drink this. Can I offer you a brandy?'

Joanna shook her head silently, numbly, staring down at the swirl of brown liquid. Cal finished his own cup, then sat back in the corner of the sofa, watching her, his fingers laced behind his head. He'd discarded his jacket and unbuttoned the waistcoat he wore beneath it. He looked relaxed, but Joanna, herself taut as a coiled spring, could sense the tension emanating from him.

She made the coffee last, drinking it down to the last drop and beyond, playing for time. As she leaned forward to replace the empty cup on the tray, Cal's hand closed round her wrist. She sat motionless, not looking at him, as his fingers stroked across the swelling mound at the base of her thumb, then found the indentation of her soft palm, and lingered.

It was the lightest of caresses, but she was as sharply aware of it as if he'd kissed her on the mouth, or taken her breasts in his hands.

To her astonishment, she could feel some of her nervousness beginning to ebb away under the gentleness of his touch.

She had fastened her hair up into a loose knot on top of her head, and he reached up and began to take out the pins, very slowly and carefully, until the whole shining mass was loose on her shoulders.

'Shake your head,' he directed softly, and she obeyed mutely.

Cal gave a low sigh of appreciation, twining a long blonde strand round his fingers and carrying it to his lips.

'You don't have it cut,' he murmured. 'Not ever.'

She should have resented the proprietorial note in his voice, but oddly it didn't seem to matter in this strange new euphoria which was possessing her.

This isn't me, she found herself thinking. This can't be happening. Yet she didn't have the energy or the will to pull away from him.

His hand slid under her hair, lifting it away from the nape of her neck, and caressing the smooth skin there in a delicate circular movement. It was her turn to sigh, arching her throat in a pleasure she couldn't disguise. She felt weak, boneless, as languorous as a small kitten. The cushions that supported her were clouds, and she was floating above them.

Cal's fingers were still continuing their delicious massage, but physically he seemed to have withdrawn to some great distance. She stared at him, trying to focus.

'How do you do that?' she asked, her voice slurring a little. 'How can you be so near, and miles away at the same time?'

'Is that how I seem?' She could tell he was smiling. 'I think, beauty, it's time you went to bed.'

'Yes.' She let him take her hand and draw her, unresisting, to her feet.

His arm was round her, and she was glad to lean against him as she walked, because the carpet was so thick, she was in danger of sinking down into it.

She was vaguely aware of another room, and a door closing behind her. More lamplight, and a blur of rust, royal blue and gold which, when she peered more closely from beneath her leaden eyelids, turned out to be an enormous bed.

'A king-size bed.' Her voice sounded wondering and far away. 'I've never seen one before. Now that is *nouveau riche.*'

'Think so?' He was laughing. 'It's also very convenient for times like this.'

She felt him drawing down the long zip at the back of her dress, and couldn't lift a finger to stop him. A fate worse than death, she thought dazedly. That was what they called what was happening to her, and she was allowing it. Cal eased the dress from her shoulders, and she felt the silky material glide down and pool round her feet.

He lifted her and carried her, and she turned into his arms like a child, feeling the thud of his heart beneath her cheek. The bed was a cloud, too, even softer than the sofa, and she sank into it gratefully, eyelashes curling on her cheeks.

She could dimly sense his shadow, standing over her. There was something she had to tell him, she thought, trying to grope her way back to awareness from her state of drifting lassitude. Something important that she needed to explain, to warn him about, but there were so many shadows now that she couldn't tell which was his—couldn't find him.

She lifted a wavering hand, while her lips attempted to frame his name.

Cal, she thought, Cal. I've never called him that.

She tried desperately to speak the word, but the shadows were too strong, too powerful, and they reached for her, overwhelming her, drawing her down into their midst, where she was lost.

CHAPTER FOUR

JOANNA awoke from sleep slowly, like a swimmer surfacing from the depths of some vast and limitless sea. For a few moments she remained exactly where she was, supine and relaxed, enjoying the warmth of the morning sunlight against her still-leaden eyelids.

She could remember vague untroubled dreams that seemed to have left her totally at peace, yet at the same time she was aware of sounds, ordinary in themselves—the splash of running water into a basin, a muted but cheerful whistling—that nevertheless introduced an alien note into the normal, familiar pattern of her awakening.

She made herself open her eyes. She took one dazed look at her surroundings, and sat up with a smothered cry as memory came flooding back, reminding her in grisly detail exactly where she was, and why.

The next thing she realised was that, apart from her dress, hanging neatly on the back of a convenient chair, she was still fully clad. And under the circumstances that seemed odd, unless Cal Blackstone had relented . . .

She turned slowly and reluctantly, and stared down at the pillow beside her. It bore the unmistakable impress of a head, so it was apparent she hadn't slept alone last night.

But what on earth happened? she asked herself frantically. She could remember feeling sleepy, and being carried, but after that—nothing. A great, dreaming void, she realised in panic.

She threw back the quilt and swung her legs to the floor, pausing as a slight wave of dizziness overtook her. She put a hand to her head, and waited for it to pass. Maybe that was it, she thought. Maybe she'd been taken ill with some virus.

She stood up gingerly. A man's robe in dark brown silk had been draped across the foot of the bed, presumably for her use. She put it on, fastening the sash with fingers that totally lacked their usual deftness. As she bent her head impatiently to enforce their obedience, she caught the whisper of a familiar and evocative scent from the folds of the robe. So he still used the same cologne, she thought, her mind wincing from the memories it evoked.

The door on the other side of the room stood half open. Presumably that was the bathroom, and the source of the sounds which had disturbed her. Moving with unwonted care, because she still felt faintly groggy, Joanna made her way across the room and peeped round the door.

Cal was standing at the basin, his only covering a towel draped round his hips. He was busy removing lather from his chin with long brisk strokes of the razor.

He turned immediately, as if sensing her presence, and grinned at her sardonically. 'Good morning,' he said. 'I hope you spent a pleasant night.'

He'd made his greeting deliberately ambiguous, she thought crossly, as her face reddened involuntarily. But there was no point in beating about the bush. She had to *know*.

She said, 'I don't understand. Exactly what took place?'

'We slept.' Cal rinsed away the lingering traces of lather, and subjected the smoothness of his shave to a minute inspection in the mirror. 'You with chemical assistance, I with the benefit of a clear conscience.'

She gave him a look of total disbelief. 'What the hell do you mean—chemical assistance?'

'You were clearly in a highly nervous state.' He applied aftershave. 'I decided you needed a good night's sleep, and arranged for you to have one.'

She went on staring at him. 'Do you actually mean that you drugged me? My God, that's the most despicable——'

'Hardly drugged.' He replaced the cap on the bottle of aftershave. 'My secretary suffers from insomnia sometimes. Her husband works on an oil rig in the North Sea, and obviously she worries about him. I asked her for a couple of the sleeping-pills she uses, and put them in your coffee.'

'You've got a nerve,' she said bitterly, remembering the cloud of weariness which had descended on her. 'They were more like knock-out drops!'

'They seemed to be what you needed.' Cal ran a comb through his thick dark hair. 'You had bags under your eyes you could have brought coal home in,' he added kindly.

'Thank you,' said Joanna, quivering with temper. 'I suppose it never occurred to you that I've been under a certain amount of stress lately?'

'I'm sure you're just as capable of working yourself into a frenzy over nothing as any other woman,' he said, shrugging bare brown shoulders.

Joanna bit her lip hard, refusing to take the bait. 'I still need to know what happened,' she said stubbornly. 'After you put me to sleep, did you...?' She paused, at a loss how to phrase the enquiry.

Cal's brows lifted. 'For a married woman, Joanna, you can be incredibly naïve,' he said, with an edge to his voice. 'If I'd made love to you last night, don't you think your body might have known about it this morning?'

Her flush deepened. 'I—suppose so,' she admitted sullenly.

'And I'm bloody sure of it,' he said grimly.

'Yet that's what you brought me here for.'

'I invited you for dinner, which you ate, and breakfast, which is on its way up—the Continental variety. I don't like heavy meals at the start of the day.'

'But you let me think...'

'The worst,' he supplied affably. 'Of course I did, Joanna. I enjoyed having you on the hook. Seeing that celebrated cool of yours melt round the edges. And all for nothing. I never had any intention of touching you last night.'

She said unevenly, 'You utter bastard!'

'Don't call me names, beauty,' he said gently, 'or I might think of one or two for you.'

'You can think up a whole dictionary, as far as I'm concerned,' she said curtly. 'I'm leaving here now, and you can find someone else to torment with your sick games.'

'You're going nowhere,' he said. 'Except into the next room, while I dress, to wait nicely for your breakfast like a good girl.'

'Don't treat me like a child!'

'Then stop behaving like one. You know as well as I do that walking out of here isn't part of the deal at all.'

'You intend to go on with this—obscene farce?'

'If that's how you wish to regard it—yes. It's what you agreed to, after all.'

'I didn't really think that you were serious—that you meant to go through with it.'

'Don't lie to me, Joanna, not now or ever. You've always known exactly my intentions where you're concerned. Your only error was to presume I was going to rush you into bed immediately, and I admit I misled you a little.'

She didn't look at him. 'Why—didn't you—last night?'

'Because you were tense, hostile and emotionally exhausted,' he said calmly. 'You were also unconscious. I prefer to wait a little longer, and hope for better things.' He walked across to her and put a finger under her chin, tilting her face up towards him. His voice was very quiet. 'I have a fantasy, Joanna, which I've been nursing for a long time. You, in my arms, warm, relaxed, and quite definitely wanting me as much as I want you.'

She drew a sharp, uneven breath. 'Then you'll wait forever!'

He shook his head, holding her gaze with his. 'I don't think so. I haven't that much patience. And I suspect you haven't either, beauty. You're curious already—asking questions, and that's good. And, if you're honest, it's been inevitable since the first time we saw each other.'

'No.'

'Oh, yes,' he said gently. 'In spite of everything that's happened in the past—the antagonism, the bitterness—whenever you and I have been together, it's always been the same. I'm looking at you. You're looking at me. Don't pretend you haven't been aware of it.'

'Your—arrogance is quite incredible.'

'Not arrogance,' he said. 'Certainty. The knowledge of who I am and where I'm going. The intangible thing my grandfather fought for.'

'Well, don't be too sure of yourself,' she bit back at him. 'I expect you've heard the old saying, "From clogs to clogs in three generations."'

He laughed, releasing her chin. 'Is that what you hope for me—ruin? It won't happen, Joanna. I'll see to that. We Blackstones have worked too hard and sacrificed too much for what we've got to let it slip away.'

'That,' she said, 'was what the Chalfonts thought too.'

He grinned at her. 'What sort of clogs have you been wearing, Joanna? Italian ones with four-inch heels?' He took her by the shoulders and turned her towards the door. 'Now run away, and wait for your breakfast.'

'I'm not hungry. And I don't take orders from you.'

He shrugged again. 'As you wish. Stay and watch me get dressed if that's what turns you on.' He began to loosen the towel he was wearing, watching her mockingly. 'Unless, of course, you'd prefer me to cancel breakfast altogether—and take you back to bed?'

'No,' Joanna said, furiously conscious that she was blushing again, 'I would not!'

She swept out of the bathroom with as much dignity as she could muster, trying not to trip on the trailing hem of Cal's robe.

The living-room, she found, had already been tidied and made ready for the day, the sofa cushions plumped and the windows opened.

It really was a most attractive room, she decided grudgingly. The previous night she'd been feeling too fraught to appreciate its finer points, but now she could view them at her leisure.

It was clear Cal hadn't opted for wall-to-wall professional interior design. The few ornaments on display had obviously been personally chosen over a number of years. Some were antiques, and others were just fun, like the collection of china bears she found on a side-table.

The pictures were interesting too, prints mingling with original water-colours, while above the fireplace hung a magnificent oil-painting of a stark stretch of moorland, lashed by rain under a thunderous sky.

Joanna wandered over to study it more closely, and it was then that her attention was caught by a much smaller painting hanging on the wall to the right of the fireplace. It was a miniature—a head and shoulders portrait of a woman, no longer in the first flush of youth, but vibrantly, glowingly beautiful, the corners of her mouth lifting in a smile, half shy, half mischievous.

I've seen her before, Joanna told herself, frowning. But where?

The little portrait clearly belonged to a much earlier era. The demurely high-necked blouse, and the thick fair hair, waving back from her forehead, and drawn into a loose chignon at the nape of her neck, betrayed that.

She was still puzzling over it when there was a tap at the door and a girl in an overall came in, pushing a trolley. There was a jug of chilled fruit juice, a basket of hot rolls and croissants wrapped in napkins, dishes of marmalade and other preserves, and a tall pot of coffee.

'Is there anything else I can get you, madam?'

Joanna's lips tightened at the sly avidity in the girl's voice. She said shortly, 'No, thank you,' then stopped as her eyes took in the dumpy figure and over-frizzed hair with dismayed recognition. She said, 'It's Stella, isn't it?'

'That's right, Miss Chalfont—Mrs Bentham, I should say. Fancy you remembering me after all this time!'

Once seen, never forgotten, Joanna thought without pleasure. Stella Dyson had worked briefly as a domestic at Chalfont House before Joanna had married Martin Bentham.

She had become convinced the girl was an obsessive snoop, searching regularly through drawers, desks and cupboards in the house. She had always been finding her things slightly disarranged, especially in her bedroom, but couldn't prove a thing. Nothing had ever been missing, but the girl's behaviour was disturbing, and it was a relief when she'd given notice instead of having to be asked to leave.

She was also an inveterate gossip, Joanna thought wretchedly. And now the whole of Northwaite would know that Joanna Bentham had not only dined but had breakfasted with Cal Blackstone, wearing his dressing-gown too.

She said, 'I didn't know you worked at the country club, Stella.'

'I've been here over two months, madam. The hours are a bit long, but the wages are really good.' She giggled. 'I'm always short of money, though.' She sent Joanna a meaning look. 'A little more always comes in handy.'

Oh, no, you little witch, Joanna said silently. I'm already being blackmailed by an expert. You stand no chance at all.

Her smile was civil but totally dismissive. 'Then you'll have to ask Mr Blackstone for a rise.' She began to pour herself some coffee. 'That will be all, thank you.'

'Yes, madam.' The words 'stuck-up bitch' seemed to float in the air between them, as Stella turned to depart with one last, malignant look.

Joanna sighed, as she drank some coffee. There was no way back now, she realised despondently. After Stella had said her piece, there wouldn't be a soul in the West Riding who would believe she was anything but Cal Blackstone's mistress. Which, of course, was precisely what he intended, she thought sombrely. He wanted everyone to know that his victory over the Chalfonts was total and complete.

'You look rather grim.' Cal's approach had been silent and unsuspected, and she started as he came to sit beside her, knotting his tie.

'I'm hardly likely to feel like the life and soul of the party in the circumstances,' she retorted.

His brows lifted. 'Not when I've assured you that your virtue is in no immediate danger?'

'I'm not interested in games of cat and mouse,' Joanna said shortly.

He smiled at her. 'No? Then what does interest you? We'll talk about that instead.'

She bit her lip. He seemed, infuriatingly, to have an answer for everything. And there was little point in continuing to be churlish with someone who refused to be needled.

She said with an effort, 'Well—I like some of your pictures.' She nodded at the moorscape. 'Isn't that by Ashley Jackson?'

'Yes. You know his work?'

'Martin's aunt gave us one of his paintings as a wedding present. I—returned it to her—afterwards.'

'Isn't that rather unusual?'

Joanna shrugged. 'It was what she wanted.' She hesitated. 'I—I was never a favourite of hers, so I preferred not to argue about it.'

Now what did I tell him that for? she asked herself vexedly. I've just provided him with another stick to beat me with. But apart from sending her a slightly enigmatic look Cal offered no comment, busying himself instead with coffee and croissants.

She hurried on, 'I was wondering who the woman was—the one in the miniature.'

He put his cup down and stared at her. 'Don't you know?'

'Should I?'

'I'd have thought you'd have recognised your own grandmother,' he said drily. 'Particularly as you were named after her.'

'My grandmother?' Joanna echoed in astonishment. She drew an outraged breath. 'What the hell's her picture doing on your wall?'

'Smiling,' he said.

Joanna's lips compressed. 'Please don't be evasive. I should have thought the portrait of a Chalfont was the last thing any Blackstone wanted around him—except to use as a focus for dislike.'

'No one would ever regard your grandmother in that light,' he said. 'She was universally respected and admired. Loved too.'

Joanna shook her head, trying to reconcile the vivid face in the portrait with the depressed and dowdy woman in the photograph album at home.

'I think you've made a mistake,' she said with a trace of curtness. 'The woman in the portrait doesn't resemble my grandmother in any way.'

'Then let's say it's how I imagine she looked, and leave it at that,' he said. 'You never knew her, of course.'

'No, she was comparatively young when she died—in her late thirties.' Joanna paused. 'My father's never talked about his mother very much, but Nanny told me once that she was expecting another child, which died, and there were complications.'

'Wasn't that rather unusual—even for those days?'

'Perhaps.' Joanna thought of the photographs. The woman at her grandfather's side hadn't looked as if she possessed much physical strength, let alone zest for living.

'A sad story,' Cal said, after a silence. 'So much beauty and charm just—snuffed out like that.'

'I think you have a rather exaggerated impression of her,' Joanna commented drily as she got to her feet. 'It's time I was going.'

'I'll call you later today,' he said. 'I've arranged for some of the local estate agencies to send particulars of cottages for us to see.'

'Cottages?' Joanna repeated. 'What do you mean?'

Cal gestured round him. 'This is very much a bachelor flat,' he said. 'You'll hardly want to live here on a permanent basis.'

'You actually intend us to buy a house—live together?' Her voice rose in shock.

'What did you expect?' His eyes glinted at her. 'A series of one-night stands?'

'Yes—no—I don't know.' She almost wrung her hands. 'Oh, this is awful!'

'It won't be that bad,' he said calmly. 'I'm comparatively well trained, and I won't stint on the housekeeping money.'

'That is not,' Joanna said between her teeth, 'what I meant and you know it. How dared you assume I'd be prepared to just—move in with you?'

He shrugged. 'You moved in with Martin.'

'I married him.'

'Yes, you did,' Cal said meditatively. 'Was that necessarily a prerequisite?'

'What do you mean?'

Cal's eyes were hard. 'Would you have lived with Martin—slept with him—if there'd been no wedding-ring on offer?'

'You have no right to ask me that.'

'I have whatever rights I choose to exercise,' he said harshly. 'We established that when you came to me last night. So, what were the parameters of your relationship with Martin? Were you still a virgin on your wedding night? Did you keep the poor bastard on ice until after the ceremony?'

'I—won't be cross-examined like this,' Joanna said unsteadily. 'How dare you——?'

'In other words, the answer's "yes".' The grey eyes bored into her relentlessly. 'Tell me more, Joanna. Did Martin know you were simply using him as an escape route from me, or did you fool him into thinking you loved him?'

'Damn you!' Her voice broke. 'I did love Martin— I did...'

'But what's your definition of love?' Cal got to his feet. 'The sort of affection you might bestow on a helpless puppy that strays into your life—caring, but passionless.' He came to stand beside her. There was anger in his face, and something else less easy to define. 'Or this?'

He took her by the shoulders, jerking her forward into his arms. For an instant his dark face swam in front of her dilated eyes, then his mouth possessed hers.

She closed her eyes instinctively, half expecting the same kind of controlled savagery he'd shown her two years before, already flinching from it, but she was wrong. This time his lips were warm and sensuous as they moved on hers, exploring the soft contours with delicate eroticism.

She stood, unmoving and bewildered, in the circle of his arms, aware, deep within her, of a slow, sweet, insidious warmth beginning to build up. Her mouth was beginning to tingle beneath his gentle, persuasive pressure, and, when she felt the questioning flicker of his tongue across its sensitive fullness, she sighed, her lips parting involuntarily to allow him to penetrate her inner warmth and sweetness.

He cupped her face in his hands and kissed her again, deeply, achingly, breathing her breath, drinking the moisture from her lips. Joanna's whole body was shaking suddenly, that strange inner warmth turning to swift uncontrollable flame as she began, almost dazedly, to respond to his kisses. The little warning voice in her brain was crying in despair that this should not—could not be happening, but her mind was no longer in command of her flesh's urgency. She had never been kissed like this before—had never known or wanted to know how it could be. Now, frighteningly, she was parched with the barrenness of her existence till this moment—thirsting for the knowledge that only this man—her mortal enemy—could impart.

This was wrong—so wrong, she thought, her mind and body reeling. At any moment she could sink to the floor at his feet, as boneless and lacking in will as a puppet. At any moment...

Cal tore his mouth from hers with a little groan, and stood looking down at her for a moment, his breathing ragged, colour flaring along his high cheekbones. Joanna swayed towards him almost blindly, her hands reaching up to lock behind his neck, as if he were the sole reality in a world gone mad.

And her need, her desire, was part of that madness.

As she moved, Cal's own hand slid down the supple length of her spine to the small of her back, urging the lower part of her body forward until it ground with devastating intimacy against his, making the layers of clothing between them meaningless.

He parted the lapels of the robe, sliding down the strap of her black silk camisole, and baring one rose-tipped breast. For a long moment he gazed down at her, his face stark, then, drawing a long breath, he touched her, his fingers moulding the delicate flesh, bringing her nipple to aching, throbbing life. Joanna cried out, half in pleasure, half in dismay, her head falling back to surrender the long vulnerable line of her throat to his mouth. He planted a row of tiny, feather-light kisses from the hollow beneath her ear down to the ridge of her collarbone, and the smooth curve of her naked shoulder.

But it was not enough. She wanted more—much more, and her need manifested itself in a tiny wordless moan.

He whispered her name against her skin, then his mouth closed on her bare breast, his tongue stroking the nipple with sensuous expertise, making her whole body shudder in voluptuous delight. Seconds spun endlessly away, creating an eternity of pleasure she had never guessed at. Never until now.

At last he lifted his head and stared down at her desire-flushed face, her dilated eyes, her mouth pink and swollen with silent entreaty.

'Is this how it was for you?' The words rasped across her consciousness. 'Did you want Martin like this, Joanna? Tell me the truth.'

What did it matter? she wanted to cry, jarred back to shamed and unwelcome reality. What could anything matter except the here and the now?

He said grimly, 'Answer me, damn you!'

'I—can't.' Even as her lips framed the words, the urgent buzz of a telephone sounded harshly and insistently through the room, and with it the last fragile strands of the sensual web that bound her snapped. Suddenly Joanna was free, standing alone, one shocked hand pressed to her cheek, as Cal, swearing under his breath, strode across to lift the receiver.

'Yes?' He bit out the word.

Hands shaking, Joanna pulled the edges of the robe together across her body and fled back to the bedroom. She snatched up her dress and dragged it on, jerking nervily at the zip, hearing something tear. She thrust her feet into her shoes, and grabbed up her bag, probing with desperate fingers for her car keys.

In the bedroom doorway, she almost collided with Cal. His hand gripped her arm. 'Where are you going?'

'Let go of me!' She shook herself free. 'I'm going home.'

'Don't run away like this. I'm sorry about the interruption. I'd left instructions we weren't to be disturbed ...'

'I'm sure you did.' Her face was burning, but with mortification now, instead of passion. 'Whoever called you has my undying gratitude.'

He sighed, leaning resignedly against the door-jamb. 'I thought you'd say that, somehow.'

'I'm sorry to be so predictable.'

His smile was wry. 'Judging by recent events, predictable is the last word I'd apply to you, beauty.'

Her flush deepened. 'Please—don't call me that.'

'But you are beautiful,' Cal said quietly, allowing his gaze to drift in unashamed appraisal down her body. 'As beautiful as my dreams promised.' He expelled a long, husky breath. 'Waiting for you, Joanna, is not going to be easy. I know that now. But I also know the eventual—consummation will be all I expect, and more.'

'Don't count on it,' she said, between her teeth. 'Now, please let me past. I want to get out of here.'

He moved out of the doorway, allowing her to pass unmolested into the living-room. 'I'll call you this afternoon about viewing those cottages.'

Her fingers tightened on her bag. 'It's too soon,' she told him tautly. 'I need time to think—to adjust.'

'Take all the time you need,' Cal said urbanely. 'And let me know what you've decided this afternoon.'

She gave him one last angry, resentful look and left the suite, banging the door behind her.

The walk from the lift across the club foyer to the exit, collecting her shawl on the way, seemed one of the longest of her life, and she felt hideously self-conscious every step of the way. But that was only a minor humiliation, compared with the future Cal Blackstone was forcing on her, she thought, her stomach lurching painfully, as she started the car and set off back to Chalfont House. This new demand of his vastly exceeded the pound of flesh she'd painfully agreed to pay him.

She crunched a gear, and, grimacing, pulled the car into a convenient lay-by and stopped, switching off the engine.

I can't go through with this, she told herself, no matter what the consequences. I know that now.

Somehow she would have to talk to Simon, and explain the pressure Cal had placed her under. His reaction would probably be violent, she realised gloomily, and she would have to calm him down, make him see that a headlong confrontation was pointless.

At least it's never worked in the past, she thought wearily. That's why we Chalfonts now have so little, and the Blackstones so much.

No, they would have to move warily, draw Cal's fangs so that he was no longer a danger to them. And the way to do that was to remove every particle of Simon's indebtedness to him, whether business or personal.

That was what we should have done from the first, she thought. I shouldn't even have tried to negotiate with him—just shown him the door. I must have been crazy even to consider going along with his outrageous demands. Crazy to think I could just—allow myself to be taken, and then walk away afterwards as if nothing had happened.

She lifted a questioning finger and touched it to her lips. But then she had not bargained for the effect his kisses would have on her, she told herself broodingly. She had thought her loathing of him, her resentment of his tactics would be sufficient armour for her against his undoubted experience and attraction.

How could she have been so wrong?

It had been a profound and potentially disastrous misjudgement, and it made her writhe inwardly to realise how narrow her escape had been the previous night. It was doubly shaming to acknowledge that it was Cal's decision, not hers, that she did not have even more to regret.

If it hadn't been for those sleeping-pills, she thought wonderingly, would I have had the strength to leave— to walk out on him if he'd touched me—kissed me as he did just now?

It was a question for which it suddenly seemed impossible to find an acceptable answer.

And that was why it was so imperative to find some alternative method of recovering Simon and the Craft Company from his clutches, Joanna thought grimly, as she stared through the windscreen.

Because she knew now, quite unequivocally, that she could not submit to Cal's demands. It was impossible—unthinkable, and always had been. Her reaction to him in the past half-hour had shown her that with terrifying clarity.

She had intended to remain bitterly aloof, scornfully immune from his lovemaking, granting him no more than the shell of her being.

But in one brief, devastating lesson, Cal had shown her that there was no immunity. Those few minutes in his arms had taught her a number of shattering truths about her own sexuality. And if she was to comply, physically, with the cynical bargain he'd offered her, she knew now she could not hope to remain emotionally untouched.

She shook her head. It still seemed unbelievable that she could have stood there like that, half naked—allowing him every intimacy he sought. And seeking more herself.

The admission made her flinch, but it had to be faced. If he'd stripped her completely, taken here there on the floor, she would not have denied him.

Her brain, her spirit, her sense of decency might reject him, but her body wanted him, as simply and completely as it needed food and water. Yet, if she did surrender to him, she would be lost forever in some destructive limbo of self-betrayal.

I could never forgive myself, she thought, shivering.

Somehow the money to pay him off had to be raised, and Joanna drew a deep, painful breath as she reviewed the magnitude of the task ahead of them.

Yet there must still be avenues left to explore, in spite of what Simon had said. They could not afford to be pessimistic. There was too much at stake for that.

There was her mother's jewellery for a start, she thought, wincing. It had been left, divided between them, and Simon had made Fiona a gift of his share when they married. But if Joanna was reluctantly prepared to sell her share, there was no guarantee her sister-in-law would do the same, at least, not without the kind of explanations Simon most wanted to avoid.

And there was no way in which her father could be approached, even in his most lucid moments, she told herself adamantly. Simon and she had agreed that his income had to remain sacrosanct, devoted to his needs, paying the wages of Gresham and Nanny who cared for him with such unremitting devotion.

And anyway, how could they confess that Simon had recklessly jeopardised their remaining security by mortgaging it to Cal Blackstone of all people? Heaven only knew what the shock of that might do to Anthony Chalfont and his precarious hold on reality.

Meanwhile, in the short term her safest, in fact, her only course was to avoid being alone with Cal Blackstone in private again.

But that was easier said than done, she thought, frowning. She would have to play a cat-and-mouse game of her own, if she was to avoid his company without alerting his suspicions.

If he guessed for one minute what she was doing, then his wrath would fall on Simon, setting in train moves to bankrupt him, so finding alternative finance—and fast—was absolutely crucial.

I'll get together with Simon this evening, she decided, restarting the car. And we'll discuss quietly, and without acrimony, what's to be done. There has to be some solution we haven't considered yet. There just has to be.

And now that she was back, she was determined to play a much larger part than before in the running of the Craft Company, where her first action would be to hire a business consultant to advise them properly, she decided with a certain grimness.

Really, we've done little more than muddle along in the past, trusting to luck rather than judgement, she thought in self-castigation, as she turned into the drive of Chalfont House. And all that's achieved has been to let us fall into Cal Blackstone's hand like—a ripe plum from the tree. We need to make ourself invulnerable against him, and all potential marauders.

To her surprise, Simon's car was parked in front of the house. Maybe she wouldn't have to wait all day to talk to him after all, she thought hopefully. But then she realised he was carefully helping Fiona out of the passenger seat, and her spirits sank, plummeting totally when she recognised the third person emerging from the car as Fiona's mother.

She had been seen too. They had all turned and were staring at the car, so it was too late to reverse back down the drive, and return at a more convenient moment.

Cursing silently, she switched off the engine and got out, aware of the inimical gaze of three pairs of eyes as she crossed the gravel. She forced a smile.

'Good morning, Mrs Driscoll. Are you feeling better, Fiona? Hi, Simon.'

'Good morning to you, Joanna,' Mrs Driscoll said coldly, looking her up and down, and missing nothing. She turned magisterially to Simon. 'I think we can see now why your sister was not available when you telephoned earlier.' She took Fiona's arm. 'Come along, darling. Mummy will take you up to your room for a nice lie-down.' She gave Joanna a fulminating glare before sweeping her daughter away.

Joanna risked a glance at her brother, and saw he was pale with temper.

'What the hell's going on?' he demanded explosively, as the figures of his wife and mother-in-law vanished into the house. 'Where have you been? I sent Mrs Thursgood up to your room to look for you this morning, and she said your bed hadn't been slept in.'

Joanna bit her lip. 'I wasn't expecting you to call,' she returned. 'I left a message that I was spending the night with friends.'

'Friends?' Simon's eyes scanned her with open scepticism. 'What friends are these, for Pete's sake?

You look as if you've spent a night on the tiles—coming home in your evening clothes!' He snorted. 'God only knows what Fiona's mother thought!'

'The worst, I expect,' Joanna said coolly. 'She usually does.'

'Well, you might have behaved with a little more discretion,' Simon muttered. 'The harm's done now. She'll expect some sort of explanation.'

'Well, she certainly won't get one from me,' Joanna retorted crisply. 'I don't have to answer to your mother-in-law for my actions, thank God.' She paused. 'What's she doing here anyway?'

'She's come to stay for a few days—to be with Fiona.' Simon's tone was correspondingly short. 'That's why I telephoned you earlier—to ask you to arrange a room for her.'

'You've invited Mrs Driscoll here—in present circumstances?' Joanna shook her head. 'I don't believe it, Simon. You couldn't.'

'I didn't actually have a choice—Fiona insisted. Anyway, if you're referring to this business with Cal Blackstone, you've surely thought of some way by now to keep him off our backs for a while. I've got enough on my plate with Fiona, and the baby coming.'

Joanna looked at him, anger stirring within her. He made it all sound so simple, she thought helplessly. She'd asked herself a hundred times since Simon's confession how he could possibly have got into such a mess. But really the answer was more than clear—sheer, selfish, unthinking stupidity.

She said, 'Simon, this is actually your problem, not mine. Maybe you've forgotten that.'

'Thank you so much.' He glared at her. 'And here's something you've apparently forgotten as well. If I go under, so do all the Chalfonts. We stand to lose everything. Or don't you care any more, now that you've changed your name?'

If she hadn't felt so sick at heart, she could almost have laughed aloud.

'No,' she said. 'I care very much. As it happens, I've been giving the matter my earnest consideration almost non-stop. And you and I need to have a serious talk.'

He looked at his watch. 'Well, it will have to be some other time. I've got to get to the office,' he said hurriedly. He moved towards his car, then paused. 'Make sure Ma Driscoll has everything she needs, Jo. You know Mrs Thursgood never thinks beyond clean sheets. I'll see you later.'

She watched his car shoot off down the drive, then turned wearily to mount the steps.

She knew what Simon was doing, of course. He was running away, trying to bury his head in the sand, just as she'd done herself only months before.

With Aunt Vinnie's wisdom and common sense to bolster her, she'd learned to face reality at last. But that was a lesson Simon still had to learn, and until he did it was doubtful whether she could rely on him for even reluctant co-operation, let alone active support.

She had, it seemed, to fight Cal Blackstone alone with whatever weapons were at her disposal.

So be it, she thought bleakly, and walked into the house.

CHAPTER FIVE

JOANNA felt better after she'd had a bath. She lay up to her neck in warm, scented, foaming water, thinking, planning and calculating.

The clothes she'd been wearing the night before, down to her shoes, she bundled into a bin liner and threw into the back of her wardrobe to be disposed of later.

She wished the memories of the past twenty-four hours could be discarded as easily, but in spite of all her efforts to blot them out they kept returning to plague her, forcing her to recall Cal's kisses, the touch of his hands on her body. And, most damaging of all, the way her entire being had flamed in response to his touch.

But maybe she needed to remember how close she had come to degrading herself completely. Perhaps that was necessary to fuel her anger, her enmity, her will to win against Cal Blackstone at all costs.

At the same time, she wished she could be sure of Simon's support in the battle. Having involved her totally in his problems, he now seemed to be distancing himself, leaving her alone to find a solution.

It wasn't fair, but, on his past performances, Joanna had to admit it was fairly typical. Simon, she thought, had always behaved as if confessing a fault absolved him of all need to put things right. He's like a child, she reflected with a sigh, and probably always will be.

She left the bath reluctantly and dressed in pale honey-coloured linen trousers and a matching shirt. She went downstairs, just in time to see Mrs Thursgood disappearing kitchenwards in an obvious huff.

Mrs Driscoll was in sole occupation of the drawing-room, glancing through a copy of *Yorkshire Life*. She looked up, pursing her lips.

'So there you are, Joanna. I've ordered some coffee. Perhaps you'd care to join me.'

Joanna pushed her hands into her pockets. 'I'm glad you're making yourself at home.'

The irony in her voice, if recognised, went disregarded.

'Oh, I regard myself as quite part of the family.' Mrs Driscoll paused. 'When I saw Fiona settled, I went to visit your father. Poor soul, he seems to be going downhill fast. I'm sure it can't be good for him, shut up in those four walls all the time, brooding about the past. He needs a change of scenery, lively company to take him out of himself. Have you sought specialist help for him? Because if not I'm sure I could recommend some very good people.'

Joanna silently counted to ten. 'I can assure you my father is quite happy with his papers and photographs. We make sure he has the best of care.'

'I hope you're right.' Mrs Driscoll gave a silvery laugh. 'He's certainly very well guarded. Your elderly nanny is quite a dragon, but I'm sure she didn't mean to be offensive.'

I wouldn't count on it, Joanna thought drily. Aloud, she said, trying to keep her voice natural, 'Nanny also regards herself as part of the family.'

'That can so often be a problem with people who've been in the household for years.' Mrs Driscoll sighed gustily. 'But as long as she confines herself to looking after your poor father and doesn't try to interfere in caring for Fiona's baby when it arrives, there shouldn't be too much trouble. Fiona's father and I intend to provide her, of course, with someone young and totally reliable, preferably with Norland training.'

'How very good of you.' Joanna's face felt as if it had set in cement. 'I hope you've talked this over with Simon. He thinks the world of Nanny and might not be too happy about seeing her supplanted.'

'I think Fiona has mentioned it, but the final decision should really be hers.' Mrs Driscoll's smile didn't waver by a fraction. 'It's a very delicate relationship, after all, and a young mother needs to have complete confidence in the person looking after her baby.'

'My mother trusted Nanny,' Joanna said tightly. 'And my grandmother trained her.'

'That's just what I mean.' Mrs Driscoll's tones were honeyed. 'I feel—we feel that Nanny's had rather too much of her own way in the past, and has come to feel she's indispensable, which, of course, no one is. But, while she can still make herself useful to your father, Fiona wouldn't dream of making any permanent change.' She glanced at her watch. 'Now, I wonder what's happened to our coffee?'

Joanna's hands, clenched tightly in her pockets, were trembling, but she kept her voice even. 'As you're one of the family, I suggest you go to the kitchen and ask. I have to go out.'

'Out again? But you've only just come home. Which reminds me...' Mrs Driscoll leaned forward, lowering her voice confidentially. 'I know you won't mind my mentioning it, Joanna, as your own dear mother isn't here to advise you, but a young widow like yourself needs to be a little bit careful about her behaviour. I was very surprised to see you—coming home with the milk, as the saying is.'

'Were you really?' Joanna felt her expression becoming increasingly glassy. 'I was also extremely surprised to see you.'

Mrs Driscoll disregarded that. 'I've never let Fiona conduct herself like that. I've no patience with the current code of morality among the young, and when there's an innocent child to be considered I think it's important to set proper standards from the first.'

'I agree,' Joanna said too affably. 'But I'd prefer to wait until the innocent child is actually here before making any drastic alteration in my way of life.'

Mrs Driscoll glared at her. 'I don't care for that kind of flippancy. I'm trying to advise you as a friend, remember.'

'Really?' Joanna raised her eyebrows. 'Then all I can say is—God preserve me from my enemies!'

Bright spots of colour burned in the older woman's cheeks. 'I can't say your time in America has improved you. You were always a spoiled, selfish little madam, with too much to say for yourself. You might remember that you're a guest in your brother's home now.'

Joanna shook her head. 'Wrong. We're all guests in my father's house. That's something you could bear in mind. Do enjoy your coffee.'

It took all her self-control not to slam the door behind her as she left the drawing-room. She stood in the hall for a moment, shaking with temper and an amalgam of other emotions.

She could hardly believe what she'd been hearing. Mrs Driscoll had always been a rueful joke to the Chalfonts. The kind of mother-in-law, Simon had once said, on whom music hall jokes were based.

But she really isn't funny any more, Joanna told herself sombrely as she mounted the stairs. The writing's on the wall, and she means business. Daddy's going to be committed to some nursing home, Nanny and Gresham are to be pensioned off, and I'm to take my dubious morals elsewhere, leaving Fiona in sole possession.

And the trouble is it could all be managed quite easily while Simon is so concerned over Fiona and the baby. He'd probably go along with anything she and her mother dreamed up.

She made her way along to her father's room with a heavy heart. Nanny greeted her, looking thunderous.

'She'll have to be told,' she said without preamble. 'Mr Anthony can't do with people barging in on him, asking a lot of daft questions, and stating their opinions. He's been right upset since she left. What's come over Mr Simon, asking her to stay?'

'I wish I knew.' Joanna sat down beside her father, and took his hand. His eyes were closed and he appeared to be asleep, although that was not necessarily the case. Sometimes it was just another method of retreating from reality. 'I'll try and talk to him this evening, but I'm not sure it will do much good. I think we could have problems.'

Nanny snorted. 'Well, this is the house for them, right enough.' She gave Joanna a piercing look. 'You don't look so grand yourself.'

Joanna forced a smile. 'I'm all right. I just have a lot on my mind. I'll stay quietly here with Daddy for a while.'

Nanny nodded approvingly. 'He likes that. He missed you a lot when you went away.'

I may have to go away again, Joanna thought. And what's going to happen then? She said quietly, 'Nanny, do you think he's getting worse?'

Nanny's bright eyes were troubled. 'He doesn't have so many good days, Miss Jo, and that's a fact, but he's happy enough when he's not being bothered, and he's with people who understand him.' She bustled off.

One of the photograph albums was lying at her father's feet, where it had obviously slipped from his lap. Joanna bent and retrieved it, turning the pages back to the old family groups.

It was really astonishing to compare the way her grandmother had been when that miniature was painted with the dowdy, lifeless-looking creature she'd become in these snapshots. Even allowing for artist's licence, she was hardly recognisable as the same woman. What could have happened to bring about such a sea-change? she wondered with a soundless sigh.

She felt slightly ashamed that she knew so little about the woman she'd been named after. If her father had been awake, she might have been tempted to question him gently, encourage him to take one of his rambling forays into the past. Perhaps she could even discover how that miniature, which must have been a Chalfont family portrait, had turned up in Cal Blackstone's possession, although she realised she would have to tread ultra-carefully over that ground.

As it was, her grandmother's picture was providing an unexpected private mystery in what had always been a very public feud, and this she found oddly disturbing, even if it was the least of her problems at the moment.

She sat with her father for nearly an hour, but he remained peacefully remote. Eventually Nanny returned, to tell her she was wanted on the phone.

I don't have to ask by whom, Joanna thought, her stomach churning as she went down to the hall, and lifted the receiver. 'Yes?' Her voice was guarded.

'Mrs Bentham?' The voice was male, but not the one she'd expected. 'This is Markham and Wilby, estate agents. We have an appointment with you to show you a cottage at Nethercrag this morning. We wondered if you'd been delayed.'

'Oh, I'm sorry!' Joanna was appalled. 'I—I'd completely forgotten. Is it too late?'

'By no means,' the voice said briskly. 'But perhaps it would be easier for you to make your own way there instead of from our office. Kirkgate Cottage is in the main street, and our board is outside. You can't miss it.'

'That's fine.' Joanna glanced at her watch. 'Shall we say fifteen minutes?'

How dreadful of me, she thought as she hastily collected her bag and car keys, but was it any wonder that my normal arrangements have gone by the board, with everything else going on in my life?

The appointment to view the cottage seemed to have been made in a different lifetime. In the year BC, she thought. Before Cal . . .

If the cottage was even reasonably habitable, she might take it, she thought as she went out to the car. Take it and put up the barricades. Show Cal Blackstone once and for all that she intended to live alone. And that he couldn't dictate to her totally.

Nethercrag was a small village, consisting of little more than one narrow main street, lined with former weavers' cottages, and a few shops. Joanna parked her car on the cobbles and crossed to where a young man, file of papers in hand, was waiting for her.

'Good morning.' He shook hands briskly. 'I'm Alan Morris. I'm so glad you could make it. There's a lot of interest being generated in this particular property, and we wouldn't want you to miss out.'

Joanna suppressed a cynical smile, yet she had to admit that, on the face of it, the cottage looked good. The exterior had been well maintained, she thought as she followed Mr Morris up the flagged stone path, and the small front garden was bright with annuals and a variety of roses, just coming into bloom.

'They're waiting for us,' Mr Morris said as he lifted the latch on the solid oak front door and led the way into a square hall.

'Indeed we are,' Cal drawled from the doorway he'd suddenly appeared in. 'What kept you, darling?'

Involuntarily, Joanna took a step backwards. 'What are you doing here?' she demanded huskily.

He lifted an eyebrow in exaggerated surprise. 'I told you I was planning to look at houses today. This was first on my list, and when Gordon Wilby told me you were being shown it this morning I decided the sensible thing, in the circumstances, was to bring my own appointment forward, and look over it together. When I explained to Gordon, he totally agreed with me. Why, is something wrong?' His eyes glinted at her in challenge.

Joanna took a deep breath, suppressing the angry protest trembling on her lips. 'Not a thing,' she said stonily, acutely aware of Alan Morris's interested presence.

Cal turned to him. 'I suspect she wanted to look round the cottage on her own, then present me with a *fait accompli*,' he said. 'I'm sorry, darling. Have I spoiled your surprise?'

'Something like that,' Joanna said grimly, lifting her chin as she walked past him into the sitting-room.

What the room lacked in size, it made up for in charm, with its beamed ceiling and old-fashioned stone fireplace, now filled with a lavish arrangement of dried flowers. A tall white-haired woman rose to her feet from a chintz-covered sofa, and came forward to greet them.

'Good morning.' Her handshake was firm. 'I'm Rosalie Osborne. These are always such awkward occasions, aren't they? I've suggested to your fiancé that Mr Morris shows you round, while I make some coffee and prepare to answer any questions you may have. Would that suit you?'

'It sounds—ideal.' Joanna was tautly aware of Cal's hand, firmly clasping her arm.

'I'm sure she'll love the cottage, Mrs Osborne,' he said pleasantly. 'Come along, darling. Shall we start with the kitchen?'

It was immediately apparent that no expense had been spared on the cottage's refurbishment. The kitchen boasted a lavish range of fitted oak units, as well as a generously sized dining area complete with traditional dresser.

'Well, my sweet?' Cal's smiling gaze quizzed her. 'Can you see yourself cooking delicious dinners for two at that stove?'

'Hardly,' Joanna returned tersely, through gritted teeth. 'Cooking isn't one of my strong points,' she went on mendaciously. 'Perhaps you could arrange for meals on wheels to be sent over from the country club.'

'No need to go to those lengths,' he said drily. 'I'm considered a fair chef myself. We won't starve.'

'That's good,' she said brightly. 'Shall we look at the rest?'

Mr Morris led the way upstairs, talking knowledgeably about loft storage, timber guarantees, damp-proof courses and secondary double glazing. Joanna let it all wash over her.

If she'd seen Kirkgate Cottage a week earlier, she would have made an offer for it without hesitation, she thought sadly. It was exactly what she wanted. Besides that, the whole cottage exuded a warm tranquillity that appealed directly to her troubled senses. For the first time in her life she could have created a home of her own.

'This is the main bedroom.' Mr Morris threw open a door with a flourish. 'Incorporating one of the property's most appealing features.'

Cal stopped dead in his tracks. 'Good God,' he said blankly.

Joanna looked past him, her own lips parting in astonishment. Greeting her gaze was an old-fashioned four-poster bed, complete with frilled canopy and looped-back curtains.

Mr Morris regarded them with the satisfied expression of a novice conjuror who had just successfully produced his first rabbit out of a hat. 'Isn't it charming?'

'It's amazing,' Cal returned. 'How on earth did a thing that size get up those stairs?'

'It didn't. When the late Mr Osborne bought it, he had it taken to pieces, then reassembled *in situ*, as it were.' Mr Morris sounded as proud as if he'd carried out the task single-handed. 'It now counts as a fixture, and provision has been made in the asking price.' He patted one of the carved and polished posts. 'To remove it would destroy the whole romantic character of the room.'

'Oh, we wouldn't want to do that.' Cal turned to Joanna. 'Would we, my love?'

There was a sudden burning ache in Joanna's throat. Avoiding the cynical amusement in Cal's smile, she moved out on to the landing. 'May I see the other rooms, please?'

There was another fair-sized bedroom, a tiny box-room, and a bathroom gleaming in ivory and turquoise. Then they followed Mr Morris downstairs, and inspected the small walled garden at the back of the cottage.

The fragrant aroma of coffee greeted them on their return.

'Please help yourselves to cream and sugar.' Mrs Osborne passed round the cups. 'Is there any further information I can give you?'

'It might be helpful if we knew what your own plans were,' Cal suggested. 'The kind of time-scale we're considering.'

'I can move at any time—in fact the sooner the better. I'm joining my sister in Eastbourne. We've always been great friends, and she's finding her large flat something of a burden these days.' Mrs Osborne paused. 'We have both been fairly recently widowed, you understand.'

'Yes.' Cal's face was grave as he glanced around him. 'It must be a wrench to give up such a lovely home.'

'Yes,' Mrs Osborne acknowledged with a faint sigh. 'Jim put an immense amount of time and effort into making it as perfect as possible for our retirement. That bed, for instance.' Her cheeks pinkened slightly. 'He searched high and low for one. He was absolutely determined—said it reminded him of the hotel where we'd spent our honeymoon. And, when he found it, he spent months repairing and restoring it. It was a real labour of love.'

'That's quite obvious,' Cal said gently. 'Was he a local man?'

'Oh, yes. He was born and brought up in this valley, and always planned to come back here eventually. It was a dream we shared, although I'm from the south of England myself. But the doctor has warned me that another Yorkshire winter will play havoc with my bronchitis.' Mrs Osborne smiled rather sadly.

There was a pause, then she went on, 'I know I'm being ridiculous and that it's really none of my business, once the sale has gone through, but I asked the estate agents to try and find me a purchaser who would like the cottage as it stands, and not want to make too many changes. Stupidly sentimental, of course...'

'And you'd like some kind of guarantee from us as potential purchasers,' said Cal. He smiled at her. 'I can state quite categorically that we shan't be contemplating anything more drastic than some minor redecoration.' He glanced towards Joanna. 'Isn't that right, darling?'

Joanna pushed her cup away and stood up, grating the legs of her chair across the tiled kitchen floor.

'I think we've taken up enough of Mrs Osborne's time,' she said, her voice sounding to her own ears strained and unnatural. 'We—we do have other places to see.'

The look Cal sent her held surprise tinged with anger as he too rose to his feet. 'Of course.' He shook hands with Mrs Osborne. 'We'll be in touch.'

Joanna was thankful to be outside in the sunlight. She took deep gulps of the crisp air as she crossed the street to her car. Cal got there before her.

'Where do you think you're going?' His voice was steely. 'And what the hell was all that about?'

'Do I really have to spell it out?' Joanna dug savagely into her bag for her car keys.

'Yes, you do.' Cal put a restraining hand on her arm. 'We could look at everything on the market within a radius of fifty miles, and not find anything of similar quality, and you know it.'

'I'm sure you're right. However, I also know there's no way I could live in that cottage.'

'Well, we're not going to argue about it in the street,' Cal said grimly. 'I could do with some food. We'll talk over lunch at the King's Head.'

'I'm not hungry.' Joanna tried to wrench herself free.

'Then you can watch me eat.' His tone was inexorable. 'Stop making a spectacle of yourself, or I'll carry you there, and give the whole village something to gossip about, not to mention Alan Morris, whose eyes are nearly popping out of his head as it is.'

Mutinously Joanna walked beside him the couple of hundred yards to the pub. A savoury waft of cooking greeted them as he pushed open the door and ushered Joanna, past the muted sound of voices and the click of dominoes from the taproom, into the lounge-bar. The King's Head was a strictly traditional pub, furnished in a way that hadn't changed for twenty years. It served hand-pulled ale, and good, homely food, and several of the tables were already occupied.

Cal settled her in a quiet corner, then bought himself a pint, and brought Joanna a glass of white wine.

'I don't drink when I'm driving,' she told him tautly.

'Very commendable, but at the moment you look in need of some kind of stimulant. You're as white as a sheet.' He paused. 'What's upset you? Surely not all that talk of widowhood?'

To her shame, Joanna realised she hadn't given that aspect of the conversation a second thought. It was almost as if Martin had never existed, she thought with angry guilt. Nevertheless, she grasped at the lifeline Cal had thrown her.

'Naturally I found it distressing,' she said shortly. 'Although I'm sure you'd prefer to believe I have no feelings whatsoever.'

'On the contrary,' he said softly, 'I have every reason to know that your emotions—and passions— are all alive and well. Although how they ever concerned poor old Martin is something we'll have to discuss one of these days. Now drink your wine, and tell me what really caught you on the raw.'

She lifted her chin. 'I've just told you.'

Cal shook his head. 'That was an afterthought, and we both know it.' He studied her for a moment. 'You were on edge from the moment Morris showed us that bed. Don't tell me it's brought on an attack of bridal nerves?'

'I'm not planning to be a bride. Your intentions to me are quite different, as you've made more than clear.' She set down her wine glass with a jerk, spilling some of the liquid on to the table.

'Is that what's troubling you?' His brows lifted in amused disbelief. 'You want a proposal of marriage?'

'No.' Joanna kept her voice low but vehement. 'For God's sake, you heard her—what she said about it. "A labour of love", she called it. You could tell the kind of relationship they'd had—that it had been good—and right. The whole cottage breathed it. And that's what she thought about us. She assumed that we—loved each other too, that we were looking for a real home together. She had no idea of the actual— disgusting truth. I felt ghastly. A sham—a total hypocrite.'

There was a pause. 'I think you're overreacting,' Cal said with a slight frown.

'Perhaps,' she said. 'But I've no intention of degrading everything the Osbornes created with the sordid arrangement you're forcing me into.' She took a breath. 'I will not live in that house, or sleep in that bed with you!'

'An ultimatum, no less,' Cal remarked mockingly. 'Do you really think you're in a position to issue one?'

'I neither know nor care.' Joanna's voice was low and angry. 'I mean it. If I have to share a roof with you at some stage, it won't be that one.'

There was another, even longer pause. 'Then we'll just have to find somewhere else,' said Cal, shrugging. 'I've got details of several other properties in the area.'

She stared at him. She was still angry, but mingled with the upset was a curious sensation, almost like disappointment. She hadn't expected him to give way so easily. She'd wanted—what? Cal to fight with her—persuade her—override her protests. She wasn't sure.

He was speaking again. 'I'll talk to the agents, and call you later.'

'Oh, spare me, please,' Joanna said tautly, and got to her feet. 'I'm going now.'

Cal rose too, his frown deepening. 'Without anything to eat?'

'I'm really not hungry.' Even to her own ears her tone sounded brittle-edged.

'Then just stay.' His eyes met hers. He held out his hand. 'Stay and talk to me.'

The hum of conversation around them seemed to fade to some impenetrable distance. They seemed to exist in a vacuum—in a small, still world of their own, the walls of which were contracting—closing in on her. Suddenly it seemed difficult to breathe.

'No, thank you,' she managed at last out of a dry throat. 'I do have some semblance of a life of my own, and I'd like to lead it while I still can.'

He laughed. 'How you do like to dramatise yourself, my sweet! Run away, if you must. I don't intend to keep you in chains.'

Not visible ones, she thought, as she turned away without replying and began to walk to the door. But there were unseen shackles beginning to weigh her down, and she was scared. Scared out of her wits.

It was simple to contemplate freedom when she was away from him, she thought, as she went up the street to her car. When they were apart, she could make all kinds of resolute plans for getting the better of him—for evening every old score, and inflicting an ultimate crushing defeat.

Saint Joanna, she thought in self-derision. Saviour of the Chalfonts.

Yet when Cal was there, she was ashamed to admit even secretly to herself, how easily he could dominate her. How increasingly difficult it was becoming to defend not just her body but her heart and mind against him.

She slid into the driving seat and dragged the seatbelt across her, fastening it clumsily, resisting an impulse to rest her head against the steering-wheel and bawl her eyes out.

It was the cottage that made her feel like this, she thought, giving it a fulminating look as she started the engine. It must be. It had altogether too much charm, too much atmosphere for her peace of mind.

She'd begun, even in that short visit, to want it too much.

She hadn't felt at all like that about the flat she'd shared so briefly with Martin, she thought, wincing. But then it hadn't belonged to them. They'd rented it from his aunt on a temporary basis, while, ostensibly, they looked for a house of their own.

Now, at last, she'd found the home of her dreams, only to have to relinquish it in the same breath.

Dear God, she thought, shivering, but it had been terrifyingly easy to imagine herself living there, setting her own seal on the place. Arranging copper pans on the wall-rack in the kitchen, placing bowls of fresh flowers on the deep window-sills, reading, curled up on her own sofa, watching winter logs burn on the wide hearth. All kinds of seductive images.

And—most of all—waking in that bed created for lovers—not alone.

She missed a gear, suddenly, clumsily, and heard the engine groan in response.

Because she hadn't been alone in any of those dreams, she realised, her throat closing painfully. Always there'd been someone else there beside her, taking her hand, tucking a flower into her hair, laughing as the sparks from a fallen log flared up the chimney. Someone turning to her—there for her, his smile reflected in her eyes. Always someone...

A car horn blared, signalling that, in her reverie, she'd drifted too near the centre of the road. Guiltily Joanna lifted a hand in acknowledgement as an indignant face glared at her from behind an oncoming windscreen. She pulled the car into the next lay-by and stopped, her heart thumping rapidly and unevenly.

It wasn't just the fact that she could have caused an accident that was unnerving her.

It was the realisation that the figure who shared her dreams was not just an anonymous faceless someone. He was one man, and one alone. The lover at her side had a face, and a name, and the knowledge, the certainty of his identity made her whole body tremble.

Because Cal Blackstone belonged to nightmares, not some weak, bizarre dream of love. He brought fear, not hope. Cold-blooded calculation, not tenderness. Peril, not security.

'He's my enemy,' she said aloud, beating on the wheel with her clenched fist. 'I hate him, and it's because of that, because of the hating, that he's there in my head all the time, filling my thoughts. There's no other reason. There can't be. I won't have it. I won't allow it!'

Her words died into silence. And in that silence came the bleak and despairing awareness that it was already too late. The conflict, for her, was over. Her chains were forged, and her destiny sealed. Totally. Inexorably.

Joanna swallowed convulsively, the sunlit day outside the car fading to a shimmering blur, as she fought the tears that would no longer be denied.

Somehow, against all logic and all reason, she had fallen in love with Cal Blackstone.

God help me, she whispered. Oh, God help me.

CHAPTER SIX

JOANNA stayed in the lay-by for nearly half an hour, oblivious to the other cars that came and went.

When she was calm again, she started the car and began to drive with scrupulous care back towards Northwaite. The self-revelation which had come to her had been as devastating as it was profound, and now she felt drained of emotion, and oddly detached.

But the new awareness had brought something else in its train: a determination to face up to a duty she'd been frankly shirking since her return. To cope with the trauma of the present by exorcising the other ghosts, other demons in her past. To acknowledge, at last, the wrong she had done.

She drove through the town, pausing briefly at a florist's shop, and up the hill towards the tall Victorian parish church that dominated the skyline. She parked outside the church railings, and, carrying her flowers, began to walk slowly up the churchyard's gravel path, her heels crunching over the loose stones.

The Bentham family plot was in a secluded corner, shaded by trees, and Joanna bit her lip as she looked down at the neat oblong of turf, with its simple headstone.

It had been Martin's own wish to be cremated, as she'd repeated over and over again in the numbing aftermath of his accident, but his aunt Grace Bentham had been adamant that he should be buried here beside his parents, and she'd allowed herself to be overruled.

The grave was immaculately kept, the flowers in the stone vase only just beginning to wilt. Miss Bentham's work, Joanna thought as she fetched fresh water and arranged the blooms she'd brought. She'd been half afraid she would find Martin's aunt keeping one of her solitary vigils in the churchyard, but to her relief there seemed no one else around. She could not have borne, she thought, more accusation, more confrontation. Not until she'd been able to come to terms herself with her marriage and the circumstances which had brought it about.

Apart from the trilling of birds in the leafy branches above her head, it was very quiet, and she was glad of it. She needed peace to think, and remember, although few of the memories would be pleasant ones. But then she hardly deserved that they should be.

'You killed him.' The words came back to her with as much startling clarity as if Grace Bentham had suddenly materialised beside her like a figure of Nemesis. 'You killed my dear boy!'

They were standing in the ugly drawing-room of Miss Bentham's house, thick curtains shutting out the daylight as a mark of respect.

The room had been stifling, but Joanna shivered just the same. 'Miss Bentham——' she had never been invited to call the older woman Aunt Grace, or even wanted to '—you don't know what you're saying. You heard the coroner. The verdict was accidental death. The pathologist said that Martin had over double the legal limit of alcohol——'

'Martin did not drink. Martin never drank.' Grace Bentham's voice was inimical. 'You must have forced him to it. You married him. You made him miserable, and you killed him!'

'Oh, please!' The words were like knives, stabbing Joanna's flesh, stabbing her to the heart. 'You mustn't say these things...'

'It's time they were said. I should have spoken before.' Miss Bentham's face was like granite—like marble. 'I watched—I saw the life, the happiness drain out of him while he lived with you. You were no good for him. Why did you marry him? Why couldn't you leave him alone?'

That, Joanna thought, wincing, was the million-dollar—the unanswerable question.

After a brief pause, the other woman continued, 'You will not, of course, require the flat any longer. I should be glad if you would vacate it as quickly as possible. I have a waiting-list of possible tenants.'

Joanna felt as if she'd been slapped across the face. She had no real desire to stay on in the flat for any length of time. It held too many memories of wretchedness and failure for that, but she thought she would be at least allowed a breathing-space, a chance to put her life together again.

She lifted her chin. 'I can be out by the end of the week.'

'Good.' Grace Bentham sounded almost brisk. 'After the funeral, I see no reason why we should have to meet again, do you?'

Even now, with the sun warm on her back, Joanna shuddered as she recalled the sheer malevolence in Grace Bentham's eyes. She'd wanted to shout a denial, to fling the accusations back in the older woman's icy face, but it was impossible.

Sitting back on her heels, she thought about Martin Bentham. Although she'd known him almost all her life, she'd always regarded him as something of a loner, always on the fringe of her crowd rather than one of its moving forces.

He'd had few girlfriends, and it was generally agreed it would take a combination of Mother Theresa and Superwoman to find favour with Grace Bentham, who'd brought him up since the death of his parents in his early childhood, and doted on him to the point of obsession. He'd been due to inherit some money from a trust fund when he was thirty-five, but until then he'd seemed content to help his aunt with her thriving antiques business.

Joanna had accepted his occasional invitations because he was always such undemanding company. Martin had never expected an evening at the theatre or a restaurant to end in bed. There had never been any pressure in his brief goodnight kisses to move the relationship to a more intimate level. She'd felt safe with Martin, relaxed. He'd been a friend who was also a man, and there didn't seem to be too many of those around.

But her encounter with Cal Blackstone on that rainswept high road above Northwaite had changed everything.

She'd felt threatened, pursued, and the kind of casual, uninvolved relationships she'd enjoyed with other men up to that point were suddenly no protection against Cal's intensity of purpose. She'd needed, with cold desperation, to distance herself from

Cal—to put herself totally and finally beyond his reach.

She could not even remember now the exact moment when she'd decided the answer was to marry Martin Bentham, but she could recall with shame every trick she'd used to persuade him to propose to her.

It had been, in theory, an eminently suitable match, joining two established local families. She'd told herself defensively that she liked Martin—she really did, and that friendship—companionship was reckoned to be a far safer basis for marriage than some ungovernable passion. And out of friendship, love would surely grow—eventually.

Their relationship might not have many fireworks, but it would be stable and secure, she'd argued in self-justification. Martin couldn't want to go on living forever in that hideous Victorian villa being fussed over by his aunt. And, as another man's wife, she would surely be safe from Cal Blackstone's machinations forever.

There'd been nothing to warn her what lay ahead of her. Nothing to tell her about the manifold complexities of human nature, or explain that there could be more than one kind of desperation.

Six months after the ceremony which had tied them together, Martin had driven his ageing sports car straight into the wall of a viaduct on a notoriously dangerous bend. He'd been killed instantly.

The church had been crowded for the funeral, she remembered. As well as the genuine mourners, there'd been the usual element of sensation-seekers, intrigued by this swift and violent ending to a newly fledged marriage.

In the churchyard, Joanna and Grace Bentham had been invited to scatter earth on the coffin. All during the service, she'd been on edge, aware of the older woman watching her, hating her. Now, as the trowel passed between them, their hands had brushed, and Joanna had found herself recoiling from the cold dank contact with Miss Bentham's skin, as if she'd touched some stone, dredged from a deep and stagnant pool.

As the vicar uttered the final words, Joanna had seen the other woman's face twist into an approximation of a snarl, her mouth parting, working as she tried to find speech. In that instant, she'd known that Grace Bentham was going to scream 'Murderess!' at her across Martin's grave. Her whole body had tensed in shock and negation as she waited for the onslaught. But it had never come.

Instead, with a cry like an animal, Grace Bentham had fallen on her knees. 'My boy!' she'd wailed. 'My darling boy!'

There had been a moment's horrified silence, then the vicar and the undertaker had moved hurriedly to her side, lifting her to her feet as she began to sob uncontrollably.

Joanna had felt nauseated, close to fainting. She'd dragged her appalled gaze away from Miss Bentham's agonised face, and it was then that she saw Cal. Impeccably attired in a dark suit, topped by a grey overcoat, his black armband neatly in place, he'd stood, as ever, a little apart from the other mourners, outwardly a picture of convention.

But, as their eyes met, Joanna had known that all the ruin and misery of the past six months had all been for nothing. That, for him, everything had been just the same, as if Martin had never existed, and that she was in as much danger as ever.

So I ran, she thought in self-derision. And I thought that would solve everything. I thought I'd be able to stay away and be safe. But there was never any safety, never any real sanctuary from him, and I knew it. That was why I came back, although I invented any number of other reasons to justify my decision.

But I couldn't stay away any more. I had to return—to see him again, to find out. And now I know—I know everything.

That was why I couldn't defend myself against Grace Bentham when she attacked me. Because I knew there was an element of truth in what she said.

I did everything I could to try and make Martin happy. I wanted our marriage to work, but it didn't, and it couldn't, because I didn't love him, and whatever I did feel for him wasn't enough—not in an intimate relationship like marriage.

I was just using Martin, and he knew it, and that was why it was all such a disaster from the very start. I was trying to build a relationship out of nothing, making bricks without straw, because I didn't dare to admit, even to myself, that Cal was always there with me, in my heart and in my mind, even then.

No matter what I did, how hard I fought, I couldn't be rid of him. I told myself it was because I loathed him and everything he represented, but I knew all the time, deep down, that it couldn't be that simple.

My God, I used to lie beside Martin at night, and dream about Cal over and over again.

Her whole body warmed in bitter shame as she remembered those dreams. She had tried so hard to dismiss them, to tell herself that they were engendered solely by the problems of her marriage rather than her unspoken, guilty desire for another man. The one man above all she had no right, no reason to desire.

But I should have been honest with myself, she thought. I should have been honest with Martin too. Then we could have ended that dreadful sham of a marriage and started again. And Martin would still be alive now.

Instead, he's dead, and it's all my fault.

Her whole being seemed to convulse in guilt and grief, and she wrapped her arms tightly across her body, staring unseeingly up through the sun-dappled leaves to the blue arc of the sky. She began to weep again, but very quietly and hopelessly, as she'd never been able to before. As she'd never allowed herself to do before.

She was shaken by sobs, torn apart by wretchedness and remorse, rocking backwards and forwards on her knees, as the storm possessed her, then passed.

She had done a wicked thing in marrying Martin, and now retribution had overtaken her. Could there be a worse fate than being made to face the unendurable fact that she was in love with a man who regarded her only as an instrument for revenge? What had he called it? 'A dish best eaten cold.'

She drew a deep, quivering sigh, and looked down at the grave, wiping the tears from her face.

I wronged you, Martin, she told him silently. I've never been able to admit that before, even to myself. But now I'm going to be made to suffer for it, so I can ask you, at last, to forgive me.

Maybe, one day, I'll even be able to forgive myself.

She got slowly to her feet, and turned away.

'I'd like a word with you, Joanna.'

Joanna hesitated with one foot on the bottom stair. She glanced at Simon over her shoulder. 'Can't it wait? I was planning to have an early night.'

Dinner had been a frankly awful meal. She was still so traumatised by the self-knowledge which had come to her that she'd hardly been able to swallow a thing. For the most part, she'd pushed the food round her plate in a pretence of eating, while her mind ran in crazy circles, rejecting the unpalatable truths still battering at her consciousness, desperately seeking a refutal—an escape, yet finding none.

Simon too had seemed abstracted, but Fiona, who'd arrived downstairs in a pink quilted housecoat that did nothing for her increasing girth, had more than made up for him. She'd sat through the meal like an aggrieved blob, complaining about her heartburn and revelling in her mother's gushing sympathy and endless reminiscences about the trials of her own pregnancies.

'I can imagine you might need an early night,' Simon said grimly. 'But I'd prefer us to talk now, please.' He opened the study door, and stood waiting for her to join him.

After a palpable hesitation, Joanna walked back across the hall, and preceded him into the room.

'Yes?' She sounded defensive and knew it.

'Paul Robertshaw called at the Craft Company this afternoon. It was his wedding anniversary last night, and he took his wife for dinner at the country club.'

'Oh.' Joanna's heart began to thump. 'I'm really not that interested in the Robertshaws' domestic arrangements, Si, and—— '

'Nor was I,' he interrupted. 'But it seems they saw you there, dining tête-à-tête with Cal Blackstone. Paul and Marian couldn't believe their eyes, particularly when you apparently left with him.' He paused. 'Well, what have you got to say?'

'Very little.' Joanna shrugged. 'That seems a fair résumé of the evening. What of it?'

'You can ask that?' Simon's face reddened angrily. 'My God, Joanna! You've never had a good word to say about him or any of the Blackstones, even when I wanted to try and heal the breach. You were the one who said he couldn't be trusted, who insisted on keeping that bloody feud going. And now you're seen in public with him, smooching in corners and worse!'

It was Joanna's turn to flush. 'I did nothing of the kind!'

'Oh, no? You forget I saw your return to this house this morning—that we all did. Where the hell did you spend last night?'

There was no point in lies or evasion. Anyway, wasn't it time Simon saw the limits to which his criminal recklessness had brought them? Joanna asked herself, as her hands clamped into fists at her sides.

She lifted her chin. 'I slept with Cal,' she said baldly.

There was a moment of silence, total, terrible, then he exploded. A torrent of furious words poured from him, violent, abusive, vile. 'Slag!' she heard as she pressed her hands over her ears, and 'Whore!'

'Simon!' She cut across the tirade, her voice cracking. 'For God's sake—*don't*——'

'You say that to me, you dare to say that, you bitch, when you've just degraded yourself—when you've dragged our name through slime! What the hell were you thinking about, or do you keep your brains in your knickers these days?'

The crudity made her shudder. 'I was thinking of you.' Her face was white now. 'You wanted my help— you needed him kept at a distance—off your back while you tried to put things right.'

'But not like that!' he yelled. 'Never like that. I didn't mean you to prostitute yourself to him!'

'Did it never occur to you that those might be his terms?' she shouted back. 'Everything has a price, Simon. In this case, it was me.'

'But you didn't have to pay it, for God's sake! Only twenty-four hours ago, you were his mortal enemy. Surely you could have made some excuse—fended him off, instead of throwing yourself into his arms like some sex-starved——'

'It wasn't like that!'

'I don't want to hear about it.' He sat down heavily, covering his face with his hands. 'It's incredible.' His voice was hoarse. 'You, a Chalfont, rolling round in bed with Cal Blackstone!' He gave a strained, grating laugh. 'And they say history never repeats itself!'

'What do you mean?' Joanna stared at him, wearily pushing her hair back from her face.

'You've allowed Cal Blackstone to execute the perfect revenge.' Simon shook his head wonderingly. 'If the whole thing wasn't so bloody nauseating, I could almost admire the bastard.'

'I don't understand.' Her heart missed a beat.

'It's quite simple.' His voice sounded dead. 'His grandfather, also Callum, if you recall, tried to rape our grandmother, the first Joanna Chalfont. She managed to fight him off, and get away from him, but that's really why he was booted out of his job, and his cottage.'

'Rape?' Joanna repeated blankly. 'But I've never heard any mention——'

'Of course not. You don't think Grandfather would have let the story get out, do you? There were plenty of other explanations for his dismissal. Old Blackstone was a born troublemaker as well as a lecher, so an excuse for getting rid of him wasn't hard to find.'

He looked at her. 'And that, sister dear, is how the famous family feud really began. Not out of industrial unrest, or local politics or even ambition, but because of an aggressive, womanising upstart who couldn't keep his hands off our grandmother.'

He snorted. 'If old Cal had possessed even the slightest decency, he'd have cleared out altogether, once he'd been sacked and evicted, and we'd have been rid of him. He might even have thought himself lucky he wasn't lynched. But of course he stayed, claiming that he was the one who'd been wronged. Every day he remained was an insult to Grandmother, and a threat as well. It wasn't that long afterwards she had the miscarriage that killed her—probably brought on by the stress of all she'd been through.'

Joanna swallowed. 'How—how do you know all this?' Her mind winced away from the ugliness of the story, and its even nastier implications where she was concerned.

'I found out while you were in America,' he told her. 'It was when Dad first started rambling on about the past. He talked about Joanna one night, going on and on about her. The whole thing was pretty disjointed and incoherent, and at first I thought he meant you. But eventually I sorted out that he was referring to his mother. I asked a few pointed questions, and finally got the whole story out of him. He was only a young kid when she died, and the whole awful business obviously had one hell of an effect on him. It made me feel sick to my stomach as well.'

'I can imagine.' Joanna was trembling. 'Why didn't you tell me before?'

'I didn't see any necessity. God, Jo, you hated all the Blackstones even more than I did! It never occurred to me that he'd try and get back at us by involving you sexually, let alone that he'd succeed.' He sighed. 'Frankly, I thought it was this house he wanted, not you. I totally underestimated his will to win—the lengths he was prepared to go to.'

She could hear Cal's voice, quiet, gloating, inside her head. 'The wheel come full circle.'

Something within her was dying, strangling in pain and bitter hurt.

'I—I can't blame you for that,' she said tightly. 'I—I underestimated him too.'

On her way back from the churchyard that afternoon, she had vowed she would make good flower from bad. That somehow she would make Cal love her in return, transmuting the harshness of his desire for her into tenderness and a caring, abiding passion.

Now it seemed that he had never really wanted her at all. It explained a great deal, of course, beginning with the miniature of her grandmother in his sitting-room. It was there to remind him of his purpose—feed his fixation. To urge him on to achieve the ultimate retaliation.

Her mouth tightened as she remembered the way he'd spoken of her grandmother, using words like 'love' and 'respect'. She supposed he was being deliberately ironical, or was he testing her? Finding out how much of their joint family history she was actually aware of?

She could understand too why he'd left her untouched the previous night. It wasn't from any kind of consideration, she thought, flinching. Merely lack of interest.

The only lust he felt was to succeed where his grandfather had failed. To wipe out that past humiliation by taking the present-day Joanna Chalfont and flaunting her before their small mutual world as the possession—the plaything of Cal Blackstone.

That was worlds away from desire, she thought numbly. It was something deeper, darker and infinitely more calculating, and she shuddered away from it as if she'd ventured too closely to the edge of some abyss and peeped into its void.

'You should have said something, Jo.' Simon spoke sombrely. 'Told me the kind of pressure he was putting on you.'

She spread her hands. 'You were so worried—about Fiona—about everything. I—I thought I could handle him.' Besides, she thought but did not say, I was afraid of how you'd react—afraid of your weakness and your anger combining into some kind of violence.

She wondered why she didn't tell him all of it. Why she didn't admit that so far Cal's conquest of her had been only cerebral. That maybe all he required for his own purpose was to appear to be her lover, rather than to become so in any physical sense.

She shivered as she remembered the sweet burn of his mouth on her body.

He'd intended her to want him, of course. Perhaps, in some twisted way, he'd even meant her to plead— to beg for his lovemaking so that he could reject her and make his triumph doubly sweet.

No, she couldn't tell Simon that. Because to confess it would be to recognise once again her own failure as a woman—a failure she'd already had to come to terms with in her marriage.

She drew a quick painful breath. In spite of all his calculations, she thought, Cal Blackstone had never fathomed that he possessed the power to destroy her totally. She had at least been spared that.

'From now on you keep away from him, do you hear?' ordered Simon

'I hear,' she said quietly. 'And if he moves against you over the money you—owe, what then?'

'That's no longer your problem.' Simon squared his shoulders tiredly. 'I should never have involved you in the first place. I—I blame myself for what's happened to you, Jo. It's all my fault.'

'No,' she said. 'No, you mustn't say that.' You didn't make me love him. That was my own private insanity. 'I'm just as culpable, and I wanted to be so strong—so clever.' She sighed faintly. 'I wanted to outwit him single-handed. But we never have—any of us against any of them. We've lost over and over again, and now we stand to lose everything.'

'I'll see him damned first.' Simon spoke with swift, bitter energy. 'He'll take nothing else—I'll make sure of that.'

'How? What are you going to do?'

He stared past her into space. 'Whatever I have to.' He got to his feet and patted her awkwardly on the shoulder. 'Maybe it's best you don't know.' His smile was forced. 'Now go on to bed, and don't worry about another thing.'

And that, Joanna thought, hours later, as she watched the first dawn light streaking the eastern sky—that was almost funny.

CHAPTER SEVEN

JOANNA spent the following day half expecting, half dreading that Cal would telephone her with details about other cottage properties. Or that he would make a concerted effort to persuade her to change her mind about Kirkgate Cottage. An unbearably painful thought.

She had no idea what she would say to him. Every scenario she mentally rehearsed sounded stilted and patently false. Maybe it would be better to come right out with the truth, she thought unhappily. Tell him bluntly that she knew exactly why he was pursuing her, and that it could stop right there.

Except that it probably wouldn't stop at all. If Cal failed with her, he might well move against the business and their home instead. After all, she had no illusions now about his capabilities—his commitment to his destructive cause. Therefore it was essential that they found some way to forestall such an eventuality.

She made a point of mentioning to Simon the possibility of finding a business consultant to advise them on the future development of the Craft Company, but he appeared totally uninterested.

'Always supposing it has a future,' was his comment.

Joanna gritted her teeth. 'Shall I make some enquiries or not?' she asked carefully.

'Leave it,' he said brusquely. 'I told you—it's now my problem, and I'll sort something out.'

Joanna remained unconvinced. Simon didn't have the air of a man with a ready-made answer to anything. He made no effort to hide his worries and abstraction, and even snapped at Fiona when she complained of feeling neglected.

Nor, it was clear, did he want Joanna resuming any kind of duties at the Craft Company. Any suggestion that she might return to work was instantly stonewalled. He and Philip could cope, she was told.

But can I cope? Joanna asked herself. I need something to occupy me. Something to stop me thinking all the time—stop me waiting for the phone to ring.

But the call from Cal did not come, either then or during the interminable days that followed. Maybe her words about leading her own life had achieved some effect, she thought. Or, far more likely, he had decided to keep her on tenterhooks for a while, wondering what his next move would be.

The weather was unpredictably and inappropriately idyllic, and Joanna spent a great deal of her time in the garden, hoping that the golden tan she was acquiring would disguise the tell-tale shadows beneath her eyes and the hollows in her cheeks which her sleepless nights were engendering.

The image of Cal as she'd last seen him, smiling at her, holding out his hand to her, haunted her constantly. It terrified her to realise how easily she'd been beguiled—how close she'd come to complete self-betrayal with him. Oh, but he'd been clever, she thought bitterly. And she'd been the fool of all fools.

While she'd been indulging in stupidly sentimental dreams of love, and a possible future, Cal's sole motivation had been revenge. He'd said he wanted her, but not even that was true. His desire for her was fuelled only by his determination to succeed where his grandfather had failed.

All this hating, she thought with a shudder. All this grim obsession down the years caused by nothing more than unrequited lust.

Callum Blackstone had wanted Joanna Chalfont enough to forget all sense of decency and honour. Balked of his desire, and publicly punished for it, he had turned in rage against her husband Jonas. If he couldn't have his woman, then he would take everything else instead. That must have been his reasoning.

That was disgusting enough. But now Cal was planning to add the final link to that chain of revenge. Herself. And the knowledge flayed her.

How could she not have seen that she was simply being used—manipulated quite cold-bloodedly? Why had she been so easy to deceive?

But then, hadn't she used Martin in exactly the same way?

She shivered. Perhaps Cal and I deserve each other, she thought wretchedly.

If her nights were bad, the days had little to recommend them either. The presence of Mrs Driscoll was rapidly making the house untenable. From breakfast to bedtime, her voice could be heard, criticising, complaining, interfering. Nothing was too minute to escape her attention, and she was constantly chivvying Fiona into making her presence felt more.

'There is always room for improvement, my dear,' she would say magisterially when even Fiona protested she could see no reason for changes in time-honoured household routines. 'You are the mistress of the house now.'

Nanny and Gresham remained unmoved, treating the visitor with civil scorn, but Joanna suspected that Mrs Thursgood would soon be at the end of her tether and handing in her notice. She wondered drily how much room for improvement there would be if Fiona found herself stuck with the cooking.

Joanna decided the best thing for her would be to try and pick up the threads of her life again. She went through her address book, making a list of contacts. During her time in the States she seemed to have lost touch with a number of her former friends. Some she found had moved away. Several were married, and even had babies. Although they were pleased to hear from her again, they all seemed busy and fulfilled in a way she could not match. The fact that she was a widow created a kind of barrier too. No one seemed to know quite what to say about Martin and her short-lived marriage. There was no one either that she could talk to—confide in. Tell the whole appalling truth about her life.

She wanted to say to someone, 'This is the point I've reached, and I'm desperate. Where do I go from here?'

But she could imagine the utter lack of comprehension—the embarrassment if she said any such thing. Instead she heard herself talking about clothes, organised fund-raising for charity, the merits of one local school against another. The fabric of lives to which she seemed barely able to relate any more. And when she escaped from each pretty colour-co-ordinated house, she would find herself breathing as deeply as if she'd just taken part in some marathon, and she would get into the car and drive up, out of the valley on to the high moor roads, to clear sunlight, the scything breeze and the solitude of her own thoughts.

Once she drove through Nethercrag. There was a 'Sold' sign outside Kirkgate Cottage. There was a large removal van too, and she caught a glimpse of Mrs Osborne supervising furniture being carried out of the cottage.

Well, she'd said that the sooner her move was to Eastbourne, the better, Joanna thought, crushing down a pang of envy. She must be supremely confident that the sale would go through without snags if she was prepared to decamp so promptly.

How marvellous to be able to map out your life with such certainty. To make decisions and keep them. I feel as if I'm in some kind of unspeakable limbo, she thought forlornly.

She got back to Chalfont House after yet another coffee morning, to find Fiona waiting for her on the steps.

'Where's Simon?' her sister-in-law demanded without preamble.

'At the Craft Company, I imagine,' Joanna returned as she locked the car, trying to suppress her irritation at the other girl's querulous tone. 'That's where he'd normally be on a working day.'

'But he isn't. That's the whole point.' Fiona spread her hands tragically. 'I've just had a phone call from

Philip, asking if I'd seen him. He sounded really upset. He said he couldn't find the current order book anywhere, and when he looked in Simon's safe, he realised the account books, the ledgers and all kinds of other stuff were missing too. Not to mention nearly everything out of petty cash.' She gave Joanna, who had halted halfway up the steps, a sharp look. 'Are you sure you don't know where he is? Philip said to ask you—if and when you finally showed up.'

'His words, or yours?' Joanna asked evenly. 'As it happens, I have no idea where Simon is, or why he should have taken the books.' She could, she thought, biting her lip, make an educated guess about the petty cash, but surely Simon wouldn't have taken a stack of ledgers to a race meeting?

She looked up at Fiona. 'Will a phone call do, or would Philip prefer me to go down to the workshops and give him my personal assurance about it?'

'Well, it certainly wouldn't hurt you,' Fiona said waspishly. 'Mother was saying only the other day that she was surprised at the amount of time you spend either mooning round the house, or out gallivanting, when there was a business to be run.'

'I'm grateful for her interest,' Joanna replied too courteously. 'As it happens, neither Simon nor Philip have ever suggested I should come back to the Craft Company on a full-time basis. I gathered, in fact, that I was totally surplus to requirements.' She paused. 'Besides, I do have things in my own life that I need to sort out.'

'Well, I can't imagine what. Simon's been like a bear with a sore head for days, and now I have Philip nagging at me.' Fiona's face was fretful. 'What's going on? It isn't like Simon to do something like this.'

'On the contrary, it's exactly like him,' Joanna said wearily. 'But if you want me to hunt for clues, I will. Is it all right if I get changed first?'

'Simon shouldn't be worrying me like this with the baby so close,' Fiona complained, following her into the house. 'The doctor said I should avoid stress of any kind.'

'It's certainly a good trick if you can manage it,' Joanna agreed drily, making for the stairs. 'Why not have a nice lie-down in a darkened room, with a little light refreshment on the hour?'

Fiona, however, was a stranger to irony. 'That's not a bad idea,' she nodded, and turned towards the drawing-room.

How nice to be so self-centred, Joanna thought with a sigh, as she went to her room. She herself was more concerned about this new turn of events than she had allowed Fiona to see. What the hell could Simon be up to now? she asked herself broodingly.

She could only pray that his mistakes and responsibilities hadn't weighed him down to such an extent that he'd decided to do a runner. That would be the final disaster.

The envelope was lying on the carpet, just inside her bedroom door. She snatched it up, and tore it open with a feeling of foreboding.

'Dear Jo,' it said in Simon's undistinguished scrawl, 'I've found a way to get Blackstone off our backs once and for all. It isn't what I'd have chosen, but there's no other option, and I'm desperate. As Nanny always says—needs must when the devil drives. Trust me, and don't say anything to anyone. Simon.'

Joanna read it through twice, with growing dismay. It all sounded too hectic—too secretive. If he was prepared to tell her this much, why couldn't he have confided in her completely—set her mind at rest?

Maybe he knows that I won't want to hear what he's got to say, she thought unhappily, stuffing the letter into her bag. Oh, Simon, what are you doing? Please—please don't let it be anything illegal!

She changed hastily out of her dress into a pair of close-fitting cream jeans and a loose violet top, and sped down to the car.

Philip was in Simon's office when she arrived at the Craft Company, and he greeted her with obvious relief.

'Hello, stranger. Any idea where our wandering boy has got to?'

Joanna shook her head, guiltily aware of the letter in her bag. 'Not the slightest. I wish I had.' She paused. 'Have you spoken to his secretary?'

Philip pulled a face. 'Jean's on holiday, and there's a temp in. All she knows is that the phone was going crazy yesterday, and this morning old Simon came in practically at dawn and pushed off with his briefcase bulging, and a carrier-bag as well.' He looked at her uneasily. 'Jo—everything is quite all right, isn't it? I mean, I'm just the salesman, and Si's the one who does the hard sums, but if there were serious problems he'd have told me, surely?'

'I'm sure everything's fine,' Joanna returned, crossing her fingers surreptitiously. 'Perhaps he's decided to change banks, or find a new accountant. He does tend to make these rapid decisions.'

'Don't I know it.' Some of Philip's tension was fading visibly. He smiled at her more warmly. 'Seriously, it's good to see you again. You look marvellous.'

After all these sleepless nights? she wondered wryly. My powers of recuperation must be greater than I thought!

She smiled back at him. 'Thanks.'

'Have you got over——?' he paused delicately, 'you know—that awful business? I mean, it must have been the most terrible shock. Martin of all people going like a bat out of hell on that particular bend, and tanked up to the eyeballs as well.' He gave an awkward laugh. 'I didn't say anything at the time, naturally, but a few of us thought it was totally out of character.'

'Yes,' she said, 'it was.'

'Just a combination of unfortunate circumstances.' His good-natured face was unusually solemn. 'That's what accidents are all about, I suppose. After all, it wasn't as if. . .' Another embarrassed pause. 'I mean, Martin had everything to live for.'

'Oh, yes.' Her lips felt numb. 'Yes, he did.' She felt a silent scream rising inside her, and fought for control, normality. She looked around, almost desperately. 'Well—is there anything I can help with, while I'm here? I don't want to butt in, of course. . .'

'Oh, but you wouldn't,' Philip said heartily, clearly glad to step on to safer ground. 'On the contrary, I was wondering if you'd like to come down to the shopfloor and cast an eye over the new finishes we're using for the kitchen units. We've tried to break away from traditional lines this time, and a woman's opinion would be more than welcome.'

That wasn't precisely what she'd intended, Joanna thought ruefully, as she followed him. She'd hoped to have a good root round in Simon's office, to see if she could find any indication about his plans, but at least she supposed she was making herself useful in a minor way.

She spent over an hour in the workshop, and had to admit she was impressed. If the Craft Company went under, it would not be for lack of ideas or enthusiasm, she reflected. The place was a positive hive of activity.

Simon, dear brother, she addressed him silently, I don't know what you're up to, but I hope you're working for us, not against us.

Afterwards they went to Philip's office for more coffee and sandwiches.

'If I'd realised I was having a guest, I'd have arranged for something more glamorous.' Philip gave her a speculative look. 'Now that you're back in circulation, Jo, I was wondering if you'd care to have dinner with me one evening?'

'That's—sweet of you.' Joanna managed to conceal her dismay. This was a complication she didn't need. 'I thought you were seeing Lindsay Armitage?'

'Oh, that's just about over,' he said briskly. 'She keeps dragging me past jewellers' windows, and leaving pictures of wedding dresses lying round the flat. Very off-putting!'

Joanna smiled in spite of herself. 'It must be.' She hesitated, searching for a valid way to excuse herself, and finding none. 'Thank you, Philip,' she yielded at last. 'Dinner would be fine.'

'Great—terrific! Have you got your diary?' He produced his own, squinting at the entries. 'I need the Rosetta Stone to decipher this lot,' he muttered. 'But next Wednesday seems all right for me.'

'And for me.' She could always arrange to come down with bubonic plague in the interim period.

'Then it's a date?'

'It's a date,' she agreed, and saw Philip look past her towards the doorway, his fresh face stiffening slightly. She thought, Simon? but knew, even as she turned to follow the direction of his gaze, that it was not.

Cal Blackstone was standing in the doorway behind them.

'I hope I'm not intruding,' he said too courteously into the blank silence. 'I was actually looking for Simon, but his office appears to be empty.'

'He's away.' Joanna found a voice from somewhere. 'On business.'

His brows lifted. 'Indeed? I'm glad to hear it. Judging by the message on my answering machine this morning, I thought he'd taken leave of his senses.'

'What did he say?' asked Philip.

'It sounded like a declaration of war, only slightly more anatomical,' Cal drawled. 'I came to ask for an explanation.'

'I—I can probably provide that.' Joanna got to her feet, putting down her half-eaten sandwich. 'Perhaps we should talk privately in his office.'

'Maybe we should.' Cal's eyes dwelled on her coolly and reflectively.

She glanced at Philip, whose expression wavered between bewilderment and apprehension. 'Er—until Wednesday, then.'

'Oh—yes, of course,' he said feebly.

She walked past Cal, her head held high, and along the narrow corridor back to Simon's office. Cal followed her in and closed the door.

There was a brief and loaded silence, then he said, 'Don't you ever bloody learn?'

'I don't know what you're talking about.'

'Oh, yes, you do.' The quietness of his tone only seemed to emphasise its underlying anger and menace. 'If you're thinking of that poor sap as a replacement for Martin, then forget it. It wouldn't work.'

'Naturally you would think so,' she said bitterly. 'But it's none of your concern, and I'll thank you to remember it.'

'Really?' He sat down on the edge of the desk, regarding her steadily. 'What makes you think that?'

'You heard Simon's message.' She took a deep breath, praying that she was right. That Simon was away somewhere, saving their necks. 'He's not here because he's arranging a financial deal which is going to get you out of our lives for good, commercially and personally.'

'Is he indeed?' He didn't look or sound particularly disconcerted. 'What's brought about this sudden rush of blood to the head, I wonder?'

Joanna swallowed. 'He knows everything—about us. I told him. And in return he explained a few things to me.'

Cal frowned. 'What does that mean?'

'It means that I know the whole sordid story from beginning to end. I know about my grandmother, and exactly why your grandfather was evicted and sacked.' She paused. 'In my opinion, he more than asked for it, and deserved worse.'

'Spoken like a true Chalfont,' Cal said sardonically.

'I am a Chalfont, and proud of it!' she flung back at him.

'Even though you claim to have heard the whole story?' He shrugged.

'It's your own name you should be ashamed of!' she said hotly. 'And your own disgusting motives. I suppose you thought it would be amusing to try and emulate your grandfather's—disgraceful behaviour. Well, the joke's over.'

'Not emulate, darling,' he said gently. 'Surpass. What I take, I keep.' His eyes swept over her without haste, from her head down to her toes. It seemed to Joanna that wherever his gaze lingered her skin warmed, blossomed. Sudden need clenched achingly inside her, and her throat closed.

She said thickly, 'You will not take me. Not now, not ever.'

'Not unless I choose.'

'It's over. I can't be—manipulated any more. Simon won't allow it.'

'What touching faith you have in that rackety brother of yours.' Cal's eyes narrowed. 'So—what's this deal he's arranging? Another Great Train Robbery?'

'That's our business.' Joanna wondered where she was finding the strength—the sheer bravado. 'But when it's finalised you'll be paid off in full.' Oh, God,

I only hope I'm not bluffing. 'And, after that, you can stay out of my life.'

'And if the deal falls through?'

'You can still stay out of my life.' Her breathing had quickened painfully. 'What you've done—what you tried to do is unforgivable.'

There was a silence. Then, 'You sound as if you mean it,' Cal commented at last. 'Which—simplifies matters, I suppose.' He reached into the pocket of the light jacket he was wearing, and extracted a familiar bundle of papers. He tossed them on to the desk beside him. 'Simon's IOUs. They're all there, but you can check with him if you're in doubt.'

'You're returning them?' She stared at him, trying to make sense of it and failing. The Blackstones fought. They didn't simply relinquish their remaining weapons and walk away. 'Why?'

'To use your own classic phrase, my sweet—the joke's over.' He sent her a light smile which did not reach his eyes. 'All done with. Finito.'

She took an unsteady breath. 'I—don't believe you.'

Cal shrugged again. 'That's your privilege. But it happens to be true. As you figured out, it did amuse me for a while to see how far you'd be prepared to go to protect the unworthy Simon. He really doesn't deserve your devotion.'

'In your opinion.'

'In the view of all right-thinking people,' he countered grimly. 'Do you think I'd have let a man treat any sister of mine—string her along—as I have you, and go on living?' He shook his head. 'I waited for him to come round—to confront me—to try and break my legs. But young Simon fulfilled all my expectations of him.'

The firm mouth tautened. 'That wasn't all, of course. I wanted to experiment, Joanna. To see how deeply that bloody Chalfont pride was entrenched in you. To what lengths you'd go to hang on to what little you have left, and protect the façade—the sham of your life.' He gave her a long, level look. 'Well, the experiment's over, and now that I know the answer I'm no longer interested.' He laughed harshly. 'But it's interesting to discover that even Simon the worm has his turning point.'

She felt as if she were dying inside, but she rallied. 'Don't—don't you dare talk about Si like that! You have no right . . .'

'It's no more than the truth. Everyone has a right to speak that,' he said. 'Jonas was the biggest bully in the West Riding, but, like most of his kind, a coward as well when his bluff was called. He never fought with my grandfather, man to man. He preferred softer targets. Your father inherited his weaknesses, but none of the iron. He was a charming lightweight at that mill, with little or no head for business, and Simon's just like him.'

'My father is a sick man.'

'I know that, and I'm sorry, but it doesn't change a thing. You've grown up believing that Dad and I cheated him—forced him out of business.' He shook his head. 'Not so, Joanna. Everything he lost, he gave away with both hands, although I won't deny that we accepted with gratitude.' He paused. 'I hope Simon can bring off a deal which will tow this company permanently out of the mire, but I'm not convinced. And even if he does buy me off, I shall be at his shoulder waiting. Don't ever let him forget that.'

'He never will.' She was hurting so much that it was difficult getting the words out. 'Nor will I.'

He gave her a crooked smile. 'I'm sure the lesson's been a salutary one. In some ways, Joanna, I'm going to be sorry you're the one that got away. I've enjoyed seeing you take the bait—wriggle on the hook. You have a very lovely body under the ladylike clothes you usually wear. I'd like to have enjoyed it—and taught you equal enjoyment.'

'The very thought,' she said steadily, 'makes me want to throw up. Will you go, please? Get out of here. Leave me alone!'

'For now, yes. Tell Simon I was looking for him.' He swung lithely off the desk and walked to the door, where he halted and turned. 'A parting thought,' he said pleasantly, and reached for her, pulling her into his arms with overwhelming suddenness.

His mouth was hard on hers, ruthlessly demanding a submission, an access that Joanna had no thought to deny him. Her clothing proved no barrier to the series of small madnesses his hands were creating all over her body.

He was not tender, yet in spite of this—or maybe even because of it?—her whole being seemed convulsed into one silent scream of yearning that took no heed of decency or even sanity. She had claimed not to want him. He had stated categorically that he did not want her. And yet—and yet . . .

Out of the bleakness of the past, the sterility of the future, this might be all she had to remember. She would make it count, she thought out of some reeling corner of her mind.

Her small hands were excited, feverish, as in turn they explored, demanded. His thigh thrust harshly between hers, and she twisted against him, moaning softly, blind, deaf to everything but her own sensual need.

Cal pushed up the violet top and wrenched apart the fragile lace cups of the bra she wore beneath it. She felt his teeth graze against the tumescent peaks of her breasts, and cried out sharply in astonishment and painful pleasure.

He froze. It was as if the sound of her voice had recalled him from some brink. Had reminded him, somehow, precisely who, what, and where they were.

Joanna found herself released as swiftly as she'd been taken. She collapsed back against the desk, staring at him. Her lips parted, soundlessly shaping his name. His face was stark, hectically flushed as he looked back at her.

Then his hands lifted slowly in front of him, as if he was defending himself, staving off the vision of some demon come to possess him. He stepped backwards away from her, his eyes never leaving her face.

He said harshly, 'Oh, no, Joanna. Oh, God, no!'

Three quick strides took him to the door. She leaned back against the desk, gripping its edge until the knuckles turned white, willing herself not to cry out, to beg him to come back to her.

She heard the door slam. Heard the sound of his footsteps retreating down the uncarpeted passage. Listened, ears straining for the sound of his car departing. Knew, when she heard it, that he had gone, and she was alone.

'It's over,' she whispered. 'It's all over.'

Her voice seemed to come from a great distance. Only the edge of the desk, bruising her fingers, seemed to have any connection with reality. Because reality hurt. Reality drew blood.

She could taste blood in her mouth, and realised she had bitten deeply into the swollen softness of her lower lip. She touched the little wound delicately with the tip of her finger, regarding the resultant red smear. It would heal and leave no mark.

But there were other scars, internal, emotional, that would never fade. And they would be her only, her lonely legacy from Cal.

That was all there ever would—ever could be between them, she thought, as the first tearing sob rose in her throat.

CHAPTER EIGHT

IT WAS late afternoon before Joanna returned to Chalfont House. She'd been driving around endlessly, aimlessly for hours, trying to make some kind of decision about her life, a plan for the future, and failing miserably. She could think of nothing but that brief, searing and hideously final confrontation between Cal and herself.

Over and over again she told herself that Cal's dismissal of her was no more than she'd expected, and that she should be thankful that he had wearied of his joke before taking their relationship to the ultimate intimacy. She'd been spared that humiliation at least.

'It's all for the best,' she kept whispering to herself, as if repeating some mantra against harm. 'All for the best.'

But although she might be able to harness her mind rationally, it was not so easy to control bruised emotions or the physical and sensual awareness which he'd so swiftly and shockingly aroused.

Her aroused and aching body screamed at her that it had been cheated of its fulfilment. And the shaming thing that would haunt her forever was that Cal, not herself, had been the one to draw back.

Joanna knew that if he'd pulled her down there and then on to the floor of Simon's office, and taken whatever he wanted from her, she would not have gainsaid him. And Cal, of course, would be aware of that too.

That was something she would have to live with.

It was a kind of perverse comfort, however, to know that he hadn't been totally immune either. That although his plan had been to manipulate and torment her, there had come a moment when he'd desired her as hotly and completely as she wanted him.

At the same time, Joanna was sane enough to realise that for her to experience the raw power of sex without any leavening gleam of love or tenderness would be traumatic in the extreme. It was no way for anyone as raw and unlessoned as she was to serve passion's novitiate, and she should be grateful that she'd escaped.

The arguments ran in circles in her head. But one thing she was sure of: if she could not have Cal's love, she would settle for loneliness, because nothing less than his total commitment to her would do. And that she knew she could not have.

She arrived back at the house to find another kind of confrontation going on. Mrs Thursgood, looking ruffled and defensive, was facing up to a clearly furious Fiona, while Mrs Driscoll played backstop with gusto.

'What in the world——?' Joanna halted in the hall, staring at the trio. 'What's going on?'

Three voices began telling her at different volume levels, and Joanna clapped her hands over her ears.

'One at a time, please,' she advised curtly. 'You'd better start, Fiona, and for heaven's sake calm down!'

'Simon phoned. He didn't say where he was, only that he wouldn't be back tonight!' Fiona wailed. 'And this idiot of a woman just took the message, and didn't fetch me to speak to him!'

'Rank incompetence,' said Mrs Driscoll.

'Nothing of the kind,' said Mrs Thursgood, bristling. 'Madam's orders were she was resting in her room, and wasn't to be disturbed for anything. And Mr Simon just told me to give the message, which I've done.'

'My own husband!' Fiona shrieked. 'You should have known I'd want to speak to him!'

'Absolute stupidity,' said Mrs Driscoll.

'I'm not a mind-reader,' Mrs Thursgood defended herself. 'Dozens of times, Mr Simon's rung and left messages with me, and no complaints.'

'But this is different, because we don't know where he is,' Fiona flung back unwisely, tears appearing in her rather prominent blue eyes. 'If I'd spoken to him, I'd have made him tell me.'

'Reliable help is almost impossible to find these days,' said Mrs Driscoll.

Joanna, seeing Mrs Thursgood's eyes beginning to crackle with curiosity as well as resentment, intervened hastily.

'There's no real harm done,' she said crisply. 'It's very naughty of Simon to be so vague, but you should be used to him by now, Fiona. Come into the drawing-room and sit down, and Mrs Thursgood will bring us all some tea.'

Mrs Driscoll put an arm round her daughter's shoulders and led her away without further argument.

Joanna turned placatingly to the irate housekeeper. 'I'm sorry about all that,' she said. 'Mrs Simon is at a difficult stage in her pregnancy, and it makes her—highly strung sometimes.'

The expression on Mrs Thursgood's face suggested that Fiona could not be strung highly enough for her, and she went off to the kitchen muttering under her breath about 'spoiled madams' and 'interfering old cats'. Joanna decided it was best to pretend deafness.

'That woman has got to go,' Mrs Driscoll stated as Joanna entered the drawing-room.

Joanna faced her coolly, lifting her chin. 'I hardly feel that's your decision,' she said. 'And I don't know who else you think we'd get to run a great barn of a place like this. Mrs Thursgood copes magnificently, and we'd be lost without her. As you yourself said, reliable help is hard to find these days.' She paused, glancing in her sister-in-law's direction. 'Or has Fiona discovered a sudden penchant for housework? I wasn't aware she even knew how to plug in a vacuum cleaner.'

'Well!' Mrs. Driscoll said explosively.

'Not the word I'd have chosen,' Joanna returned. 'If Mrs Thursgood leaves, you'll be in real trouble, I promise, especially from Simon, who adores her cooking.' She paused. 'And it might be better, Fiona, if you were a bit more discreet about Simon's absence until we find out where he's gone and why. I'm sure you don't want to start a rumour that he's left you.'

'You're being horrid. He hasn't,' Fiona said tearfully.

'Probably not, though I can't say I'd blame him if he had,' Joanna retorted. 'He has all the worries of the business to cope with, and not a particularly comfortable home life to come back to, with your non-stop whinging, among other things,' she added with a grim sideways glance at Mrs Driscoll.

Fiona sat bolt upright on the sofa. 'Joanna—you've never spoken to me like this before!'

'No, I haven't,' Joanna said affably. 'But I've wanted to—many times. It's time you got a grip, Fiona, on yourself and your marriage.' And your mother, she added silently as she walked to the door. 'Now I'm going up to sit with my father. I don't want to spoil your tea-party any further.'

She felt marginally more cheerful as she walked upstairs. If she'd persuaded Fiona to pause, even for a second, and take stock of her life, then she might have done Simon a favour. I only hope he deserves it, she thought with a sigh, as she went along to her father's room.

Anthony Chalfont was lying back in his chair, his eyes closed, breathing stertorously.

'How is he today, Nanny?' Joanna asked in a low voice.

Nanny pursed her lips. 'Not so good, Miss Jo, and that's a fact. He didn't seem to know Gresham at all this morning, and he didn't want his lunch. Let the whole tray tip on to the floor, just like when he was a toddler. And he hasn't had a word to say all afternoon. It's as if he can't hear what's said to him—or won't.'

'Oh, dear.' Joanna bit her already sore lip, and winced. 'I'll stay with him for a while, so that you can have a break.'

'Just as you like, my dear. I'll go and see if the evening paper's come yet.'

Joanna fetched her usual low padded stool, and seated herself beside her father, resting her head against the arm of his chair. It was time, she thought, that she and Simon faced up to the fact that her father's condition wasn't just a deliberate retreat from unpleasant reality, but was medical in origin. Her mind shied away from the more obvious possibilities. However, it seemed clear that in the near future he would need more specialised and stringent care than Nanny or Gresham could provide.

Once I would simply have blamed the Blackstones, and the loss of the mill, she thought wearily. So I suppose I'm making progress.

Cal's harsh words about her father had hurt, but she was forced to admit they held a certain amount of justice. Other people, she recalled, had said or hinted much the same over the years, although she had chosen to disregard their comments. Anthony Chalfont had been brought up to enjoy a certain life-style and a definite inheritance. He was no battler for his share of the market-place, and these days one had to be, especially in the woollen industry, she reflected sadly.

The loss of her mother had wrought a profound effect on him too. Cecilia's had been a strong, forceful personality, not always comfortable to live with, but certainly one to be missed.

She sighed. Whatever curse old Callum Blackstone had put upon the Chalfonts, it seemed to have had its effect over the years. And where was the justice in that? Jonas Chalfont, after all, and his wife had been the injured parties.

She got up quietly and fetched the photograph album, turning the pages with renewed curiosity. Had an attempted rape really had the power to turn the vibrant Joanna Chalfont into this depressed, dowdy woman? Surely not, yet there seemed no other answer to the enigma. Studying the photographs of her grandfather, she couldn't imagine him being particularly caring or supportive in such a situation. Perhaps he was one of those husbands who believed there was no smoke without fire, and that his wife had brought her disgrace on herself by her own conduct, she thought, grimacing.

She had no sympathy at all for such an attitude, but then neither could she understand Cal's obvious support for his own grandfather in view of what he'd tried to do. Unless he too believed that Joanna had led Callum on.

She remembered the merry, beautiful face in the miniature. Was that really the kind of woman who teased a man beyond bearing, then tried to draw back at the last moment? It wasn't easy to believe. But the fact that Callum Blackstone had the miniature in his possession suggested that her grandmother had encouraged him to a certain extent.

She must have given it to him, Joanna mused, because if he'd stolen it, then Jonas would undoubtedly have had him charged with theft. She shook her head vexedly. The more she thought about it, the more bewildering it all became.

But then everything was such a mess, and had been from the start. Cal might have repudiated her, but that didn't mean the feud was over. 'I'll be waiting,' he'd threatened.

Joanna closed her eyes, feeling the ache of tears in her throat. She would have to go away from the Valley. She had no choice. She couldn't stay and see the man she loved destroy the brother she'd always had to protect. Nor could she shield Simon any more. She'd tried, and it had been a total disaster.

I shouldn't have interfered, she thought drearily. I should have come back, seen what the situation was, and taken off again. But I expected to find Cal safely married, and the feud reduced to a state of armed neutrality at worst. I wanted an anticlimax, not a crisis.

She wondered exactly how she would have felt if she'd indeed returned to find Cal with a wife. If then she would have recognised her enmity, her inimical opposition to him for what it really was—the obverse side of love?

As it was, it hadn't taken long for the truth to dawn on her. And now she had to bear the burden of that truth for the rest of her life.

Anthony Chalfont stirred in his uneasy sleep, and muttered something. Joanna clasped his fingers in her own, and he subsided again.

In some ways she could be thankful that she hadn't been called on to make the inevitable choice between her family and her lover. Safe in his twilight world, her father would never know how close she'd come to betraying the Chalfont name.

The Montagues and Capulets have nothing on us, she thought with self-derision. I'd have found myself cut off with the proverbial shilling and deleted from the family Bible.

But I might have settled for that if only Cal had loved me.

'You can't love him,' said Anthony Chalfont. 'You can't leave us.'

For one stricken moment, Joanna wondered if she'd spoken her unhappy thoughts aloud. But she knew that was impossible.

Her fingers tightened on his. 'It's all right, darling.' She made her voice soothing. 'I'm here. I'm not going anywhere. It's all right.'

His eyes were open, searching her upturned face with total incomprehension.

'Don't go, Mummy,' he said. His hand clung painfully to hers. 'Stay with me, please. Say you love me best, better than him. Please, Mummy!'

A long, icy shiver passed down Joanna's back. When he looked at her, what was he seeing? A woman with fair hair drawn back from her face. But a face from the past rather than the present.

She said softly, 'It's all right, darling. What makes you think I'm leaving?'

'I heard,' he said. 'I heard you and Father last night. He was shouting. I hate it when he shouts.'

Joanna's heart missed a beat. 'What did you hear?' She tried to keep her voice level.

'He said he'd see you dead before you went to him. And he'd turn him and his other brat into the gutter to starve. What did he mean?'

'Father was just angry,' Joanna said quietly. Other brat? she thought, suddenly aware that Nanny was standing in the doorway, as still as if she'd been turned to stone. 'People say terrible things when they're angry, but they don't mean them.'

'Father means them.' Anthony Chalfont's voice sounded dead, exhausted. 'He always means them. Don't leave me with him.'

'No,' she said. 'No, I won't. Try and sleep now.'

He gave a long, defeated sigh and closed his eyes again. Gradually his grip on her hand relaxed, and she was able, gently, to extricate herself.

Nanny closed the door, her expression grim. 'What brought that on?' she asked, as she came over to Mr Chalfont's chair. 'Have you been upsetting him, Miss Jo, prying into things best forgotten?'

'Best forgotten?' Joanna's brows lifted. 'How on earth can you say that? We were just sitting here, and he began talking, begging me not to leave. He obviously thought I was his mother.'

'He's always confused at this time of day.'

'He seemed perfectly rational to me.' Joanna said evenly. 'This was something from his childhood he was remembering. Some terrible, traumatic thing. You were his nanny. I'm sure you would have known what was going on.'

'Leave the past be, Miss Jo. You'll do no good by raking over the ashes . . .'

'I'll be the judge of that.' Joanna paused for a moment, collecting her whirling thoughts. 'Simon told me that Callum Blackstone tried to rape my grandmother, but that isn't true, is it? She was in love with him. She was planning to go away with him and Grandfather found out. He made her stay, and that's why she changed so much in the photographs.'

'Photographs?' Nanny shook her head. 'You'll find no photographs of her in this house, Miss Jo. He took every last one and burned them after she—she . . .

Haven't you ever wondered about all the gaps in them albums?'

'Well—yes.' Joanna retrieved the leather-bound book from the carpet at her feet. 'Then who's the woman beside Grandfather in all these pictures?'

'That's your grandfather's sister. Myra, they called her. She came to keep house for him—afterwards. Ended up marrying the Methodist minister and going off to some mission station. Said even if there were cannibals, they couldn't be worse than your grandfather.'

Joanna swallowed. 'Was he that bad?'

'He was a hard man, Miss Jo, and cold as winter. He never needed a human wife, he was married to that damned old mill of his. Work was all he ever thought of, and making more money. And she——' Nanny's face was gentle, suddenly, and sad. 'Ah, but she were lovely, and no one ever said different. She had all the warmth and joy in her that he lacked. Living with her might have softened him, but it didn't. He left her alone too much, especially after your dad was born. She had nowt to do but rattle around in this house, and it weren't enough, so she took up with charity work.'

'And met Callum Blackstone?'

'I've said enough.' Nanny's lips tightened. 'It's not for me to judge her, anyway. I thought the world of her. I only stayed here to look after your dad because she begged me. She didn't want him turning the boy against her after she'd died. But it was Callum Blackstone he poisoned your dad's mind with, repeating the same old lies over and over again, making Mr Anthony believe them. Maybe he even came to believe them himself, after a time. It seemed to me he was a man who enjoyed hating—your grandfather. But hatred destroys in the end, and he never understood that.'

'My God!' Joanna said unsteadily. 'Why did you let me grow up thinking...? Why didn't you tell us the truth, Simon and me?'

'Because it wasn't my place,' Nanny said firmly. 'I wouldn't have spoken now, but for Mr Tony saying those things. He must have had them tucked away at the back of his mind since he was a little lad.'

'I suppose so,' Joanna said. There was a tightness in her chest. 'There's one more thing I have to know, Nanny.' She paused, taking a deep breath. 'My grandmother—did she die of natural causes?'

Nanny looked shocked. 'Oh, aye, Miss Jo, it was natural enough. Just one of those sad things that doctors can't explain. She lost the baby, and just seemed to—fade.' She shook her head again, her face wistful. 'No, your grandfather wasn't a violent man—not in that way. You mustn't ever think that. But there was no kindness in him, no forgiveness, and maybe she knew the sort of life she could expect from then on.' She sighed. 'He'd have given her hell on earth, Miss Jo. Hell on earth. So perhaps she didn't fight too hard at the end.'

'We should have been told, Simon and I.' Joanna beat her clenched fist into the palm of the other hand. 'We shouldn't have grown up believing all those lies—adding to the hatred, the misunderstanding.'

'Well, it's in your hands now, Miss Jo. Maybe you could do something to heal the breach, if you wanted.' Nanny sent her a shrewd look. 'Vera Thursgood was saying there'd been talk lately, linking you with a certain other person...'

Joanna forced frozen lips to smile. 'Well, Mrs Thursgood shouldn't believe everything she hears. I'm afraid there'll be no healing done.' She bent and dropped a kiss on her father's hair. 'It's too late for that.'

Too late, she thought, as she went slowly back to the solitude of her own room. Much, much too late.

It was not a pleasant evening. Dinner was served by Mrs Thursgood with a certain amount of clashing of crockery. Mrs Driscoll appeared on the point of speaking her mind several times, but subsided after receiving a minatory look from Fiona.

Joanna, observing this with detached interest, wondered if her strictures had borne fruit after all. She herself was regarded warily by both women, as if she were a hand grenade which might or might not explode. When the meal was over, she accompanied them to the drawing-room, and sat in dutiful silence through a series of nondescript television programmes, while Mrs Driscoll, occupying the sofa in an almost tangible aura of disgruntlement, added a crochet edging to the matinee coat she had just completed.

It was frankly a relief to Joanna when she could announce her intention of having an early night, and retire upstairs.

She had not expected to sleep, and yet she found her eyelids were closing almost as soon as her head touched the pillow. Her dreams were fleeting, elusive, disturbing. Always she seemed to be searching for something that remained just beyond her reach.

When she felt a touch on her shoulder, she was awake in an instant. 'It still feels like the middle of the night,' she yawned, lifting herself on to an elbow.

'It is the middle of the night, Miss Jo.' It was Nanny who'd woken her, and beyond her Mrs Thursgood was hovering in the doorway. 'Can you come downstairs a minute? There's been some trouble at the Craft Company. A policeman would like to have a word with you.'

'Oh, God!' She was out of bed immediately, reaching for her robe and thrusting her feet into slippers.

The policeman was waiting in the drawing-room. He was big and fair and serious-looking.

'I'm afraid I've got some bad news for you, madam,' he said. 'There's been a fire at your workshops.'

'Oh, no!' Joanna ran her tongue round suddenly dry lips. 'Has it done much damage?'

'I'm afraid so. It had got a good hold by the time the alarm went off, although someone had reported it before then.' He paused. 'It was actually Mr Simon Chalfont I wanted to have a word with, but your housekeeper informs me he's not expected home tonight.'

'That's right.' Joanna kept her voice calm. 'But his partner, Mr Philip Driscoll, is available . . .'

'Oh, we've been in touch with Mr Driscoll. He's been down at the scene of the fire for the past hour, together with Mr Callum Blackstone, who's got a major financial interest, I understand.'

'Why—yes,' Joanna said slowly. 'But that isn't generally known. Who contacted him?'

'No one, madam. He's the one who reported the fire in the first instance. He happened to be driving past and realised something was wrong.'

'I—see,' Joanna said slowly and untruthfully. 'How fortunate.'

'Joanna?' Fiona's voice sounded from the doorway. 'What's going on? What's wrong?' Her eyes widened as she saw the policeman. 'Oh!' Her hand went up to clutch at her throat. 'It's Simon, isn't it? There's been some terrible accident...'

'No, of course not.' Joanna moved to her side.

'Oh, thank heavens!' Fiona looked at the policeman. 'I've been so worried, officer. My husband simply vanished today, and none of us knows where he is. You couldn't find him for me, I suppose?'

'Not unless he's been reported as a missing person, madam, and that would seem slightly premature.' But the policeman was frowning.

Joanna intervened swiftly. 'My brother's away on business, officer. He tends to be a little vague about his movements sometimes.'

'So what has happened?' Fiona demanded.

'There's been a fire at the Craft Company—a pretty extensive one,' Joanna told her.

'Oh, is that all?' Fiona shrugged her shoulders.

'All?' Joanna was appalled. 'Fiona—our business premises have been just about destroyed.'

'But the insurance will cover it. Simon increased it only recently. He told me so.'

There was a silence. The policeman's frown deepened. 'Did he indeed, madam? Well, that was very far-sighted of him. Quite providential, in fact. Let's hope that any claim that's made is perfectly straightforward.'

'Is there any reason why it shouldn't be?' Joanna did her best to sound casual, but her heart was thudding uncomfortably.

The policeman gave her a long, unwavering look. 'There's some evidence that a fire was deliberately started on the premises, madam, so naturally there will have to be a strict investigation. That's why Mr Blackstone disclosed his financial interest in the company to us. Quite understandably, he wishes to be kept fully informed about our enquiries.' He paused. 'Perhaps you can see now, madam, why we're so keen to have a word with Mr Simon Chalfont.'

Simon's words came floating back into Joanna's head. 'He'll take nothing else—I'll make sure of that.' He'd said he'd do whatever he had to, she thought numbly. He'd said he was desperate. The room swayed around her.

Needs must when the devil drives.

Fiona gave a shrill laugh. 'Good heavens, constable! You surely don't think my husband burned down his own business?'

The room was spinning now, faster and faster, out of control. When the devil drives, thought Joanna, and fainted.

CHAPTER NINE

THERE was darkness all around Joanna. Her eyelids felt weighted and she struggled feebly to open them.

'Take it easy,' a voice said. 'Relax. It's all right.'

There were fingers clasping hers, holding them tightly, pulling her back from the all-pervading blackness. She looked up into Cal's face. He looked weary and grimy, and the smell of smoke hung around him.

She said absurdly, 'It's you.' Then, 'I feel sick.'

'Lie still,' he told her. 'It will pass.'

She was lying on the drawing-room sofa, she discovered. Over his shoulder she could see Philip looking equally dishevelled, and Fiona, wide-eyed and twittering.

'What happened?' she asked dazedly.

'You passed out. Driscoll and I walked in, and found you stretched on the carpet, with Mrs Chalfont having hysterics over you, and a young bobby trying to bring you round.'

'I remember,' she said slowly. She was beginning to remember altogether too much. Why the policeman had been there, and what Fiona had said, just before the darkness closed in. Simon, she thought, desperately. Oh, Simon. 'The policeman—where is he?' She tried to sit up, but Cal pushed her quietly but firmly back against the cushions.

'He's just gone. He'll come back later.'

'Will he?' Her eyes searched his face, looking for a comfort she didn't find. 'Is—is the fire bad?'

'About as bad as it could be. The smoke detectors couldn't have been working as well as they should be.'

Or they'd been tampered with. The unspoken comment seemed to hover in the room.

After a pause, Cal went on, 'It will all have to be gone into, naturally.'

'All that stuff,' Philip muttered. 'All those completed orders. God, this is a disaster!'

'But we're insured,' Fiona insisted. 'Heavily insured. Simon told me we were. The insurance will pay.'

Joanna moved restively, and Cal looked down at her.

He said, 'It's time we all tried to get some sleep. Can you walk to your room?'

She swung her legs to the floor, and stood. The room swam. Cal's arm was there, suddenly, like an iron bar supporting her.

'Obviously not.' He picked her up in his arms as if she were a child, and started for the door.

'Now just a minute,' Philip began hectoringly. 'I don't know what gives you of all people the right to march in here and take over——'

'We'll discuss that in daylight. In the meantime, look after your sister. This must have been a shock for her.' Cal eyed him coldly, and Philip subsided, reddening.

Cal carried Joanna out into the hall, and towards the stairs. Under her cheek, the thud of his heart was firm and steady. Her own pulses were going haywire, and she was trembling deep inside. How could he not know? she thought. How could he not care?

'You'll have to direct me,' he said as they went up the stairs.

'It's to the left. The second door along.' Her voice sounded small and shaky.

He shouldered his way in with her, and put her down on the bed, with an impersonal efficiency that chilled her. He'd carried her before, she thought, but that had been in some other age, some other existence.

'Try and rest,' he directed brusquely. As he straightened, she put a hand on his arm, gripping his sleeve.

Don't leave me. The words rose to her lips and had to be bitten back. Instead she said, 'What's going to happen?'

'There'll be an investigation—a full inquiry. The insurance company will insist.' His expression was unreadable.

Joanna bit her lip. 'There's no way it can be avoided?'

'None. It's out of our hands.' He looked at her, his mouth tightening. 'Are you going to be all right? Shall I ask someone to come and be with you?'

'I'm fine,' she lied. She gave a small, strained laugh. 'I've never fainted in my life before. That's usually Fiona's prerogative.'

He didn't smile back at her. 'Try not to worry too much. There's nothing you can do. It's just one of those things.' He detached her fingers from his sleeve, gently but very definitely. 'I must go. I'll—see you around.'

She nodded, suppressing the sob rising in her throat, as he walked away from her to the door. His whole attitude was making it clear she had nothing to hope for from him. He'd meant every word he'd said at their last meeting.

Cal went out and didn't look back.

Joanna lifted her clenched fist and pressed it against her lips. So—that was it. It was all over. He was distancing himself while they drowned in a new sea of troubles. But what else did she expect? she asked herself wearily. He was hardly likely to leap to Simon's aid again—not after last time.

But I can't let him go—just like that, she argued with herself. There's so much I haven't told him—so much I need to say. He doesn't know, for instance, that I've found out the truth about our grandparents. I must tell him that, at least. He has a right to know.

She got off the bed and went to the door, stumbling a little over the hem of her dressing-gown. As she made her way along the gallery to the head of the stairs, she heard his voice in the hall below.

'No,' he was saying, 'there's no doubt at all—the fire was started quite deliberately. All the evidence is there.'

'Have they any idea who's responsible?' Philip's voice was strained and worried.

Joanna felt the breath catch in her throat as she listened.

'I think they're almost certain,' Cal said grimly. 'It's just a question of finding him, and getting the truth out of him.' He paused. 'If Simon should happen to show up here, tell him to get in touch with me immediately. It's most urgent.'

'Yes,' Philip said heavily. 'Yes, I understand.'

A moment later the front door banged, and she heard Philip go back into the drawing-room, talking too loudly and cheerfully to Fiona.

Joanna shrank back against the wall. All her worst fears were being confirmed. It was like a bad dream come true.

Arson, she thought. And Simon had done it. *Simon.* He'd burned down the Craft Company for the insurance. What was more, his guilt was known. When he returned, he would be interviewed and arrested. And if he was convicted, he would probably be sent to prison.

She felt sick again. The fool, she thought, hugging her arms across her body. The idiot! How on earth could he have imagined he'd get away with it? But of course, she reminded herself grittily, Simon didn't think things through. That was why he was in his present financial mess.

She went slowly back to her room and got under the covers of the bed, still in her dressing-gown, shivering as if she would never be warm again.

What was going to happen to them all? she wondered wretchedly. They would lose the house, of course. That went without saying. Cal would take it to recoup his losses. Her father would be robbed of his only sanctuary. Simon's life would be wrecked and his marriage, such as it was, ruined.

If only he'd given her some idea—some hint of what he was planning. Maybe she could have talked him out of it. I should have guessed from the way he spoke that he had something totally crazy in mind, she castigated herself.

Oh, Si, I won't be able to rescue you this time.

Two lonely people had found love and a brief happiness together, and from this two generations of disaster had sprung. Where would it all end? she asked herself desolately.

But she could find no answer as she lay tossing and turning through what remained of the night.

'I wish old Si would come back,' Philip grumbled. It was the umpteenth time he'd said it, and Joanna felt her teeth gritting automatically.

This had been one of the longest days of her life, she thought. The phone had never stopped ringing. Mostly it was friends and acquaintances calling to exclaim and condole, but sometimes it was the Press who'd got wind of the arson rumour, and were much trickier to fob off with 'No comment'. And twice it had been the police asking politely if Mr Chalfont had yet returned, or if there had been any word from him. Again the reply to both questions was in the negative. But for how long would they continue to take 'no' for an answer?

At least Fiona was out of the way, she thought. Mrs Driscoll had borne her off to Harrogate, babyshopping, 'to take her mind off things'. Not that Fiona seemed unduly troubled. Simon's continuing absence made her fretful rather than genuinely anxious. Clearly the deeper implications of the situation were lost on her.

Lucky Fiona, Joanna thought wryly.

Cal had not phoned. There had not been a sign or a message from him all day. But then, what had she really expected?

'See you around.' That surely had to be the most laconic of dismissals.

Needless to say, her father had been disturbed by the comings and goings in the night.

'You'd best tell him the truth, Miss Jo,' Nanny had advised. 'It'll only fret him otherwise.'

I'll tell him part of it, Joanna thought wearily. The whole truth would fret him far more.

Aloud, she said, 'Do you think he can take it?'

'For all he hasn't slept, he's grand this morning,' Nanny told her. 'Right as a bobbin.'

To her amazement, Anthony Chalfont had accepted the news that the Craft Company was now a blackened ruin quite calmly. The bewildered child remembering his mother and an old tragedy might never have existed. He seemed his old self again. Joanna found herself wondering if allowing himself to remember the truth, voicing those early fears and traumas about his mother, had proved some kind of catharsis for him.

'This fire is only a temporary setback.' He sat straight-backed in his chair, his hands folded tranquilly in his lap. 'Simon will have to deal with it as such—find alternative premises while we rebuild. Has he done so yet?'

Joanna hesitated. 'Simon's away on business at the moment. We haven't been able to contact him yet.'

'Simon will look after things.' Her father looked over the sunlit gardens. 'There was a time, Joanna, when I thought you should have been born the boy. But Simon's doing well now. I have great faith in him.' He nodded, smilingly. 'Great faith.'

'That's good,' she said, biting her lip. 'That's fine.'

Or it would be until Simon came out of hiding and gave himself up, she'd thought grimly. What would the shock of that do to her father? Send him back into some vague and clouded past again? She couldn't bear that.

Now she looked at Philip. 'There's really no need for you to wait here,' she said. 'I'm sure you must have a million things to do.'

Philip pursed his lips. 'Can't really make many decisions without old Si.' He shook his head. 'Should have told us where he was going. Makes things very difficult when we don't know.'

Joanna looked down at the floor. 'How do you think the fire started, Philip? What have the police told you?'

'Damned little.' Philip looked vaguely sullen. 'It's Blackstone they confide in, not me. He seems to have taken over completely. Quite extraordinary.' He gave a slight cough. 'I knew that he and Simon had done business in some marginal way, but I didn't realise he was now a regular visitor here.'

'He isn't,' Joanna said briefly.

'Oh?' Philip raised his eyebrows. 'Well, he seemed perfectly at home last night, Joanna. There's been a few rumours around, I don't mind telling you. I've always dismissed them as rubbish, but the way he came marching in here as if he owned the place made me think a bit. Not to mention his arrival at the Craft Company yesterday.'

Joanna gave him a constrained smile. 'He doesn't own this house, I can assure you.' Not yet, anyway.

Philip looked faintly sceptical. 'There was a time when a Blackstone wouldn't have been allowed across the doorstep.'

'Perhaps,' Joanna said evenly. 'But feuds are such a waste of time, and like most quarrels no one can ever really remember how they began.'

'I see,' said Philip, as if he did. 'Well, I felt I had to ask. After all, if we're going to be seeing something of each other...'

Joanna stared at him. 'I agreed to have dinner with you,' she said, 'nothing more.'

'Oh, naturally,' Philip said hastily. 'But all the same, you can't deny it would be altogether a bad thing if we decided in due course...' He stumbled to a halt. 'I mean, Si and Fiona would be delighted.'

'Your mother too,' Joanna agreed, dead-pan, while inwardly she recoiled, shrieking.

'Oh—er—yes.' For a minute he looked totally blank, to Joanna's secret delight. But this was a line of conversation she had no wish to encourage, she decided. She reached for her bag. 'If you'll excuse me for a while, Philip, I think I need some air.'

'You're going out? But what if Simon rings?'

Joanna shrugged, evincing a nonchalance she was far from feeling. 'Then he can leave a message. After all, we can't sit here forever waiting for his call.'

'I suppose not,' Philip agreed reluctantly. 'But I think I'll hang on here, if that's all right. In case something crops up,' he added uneasily.

'Please do,' Joanna said cordially.

She drove straight to the Craft Company, and parked, staring in frank disbelief through the windscreen. Although she'd been warned what to expect, she still hadn't anticipated quite this level of damage. All that remained of the building was a blackened shell.

She left the car and began to walk towards the ruin. There were other onlookers around as well, she noticed. The air was still acrid, and she coughed slightly, putting her hand over her mouth.

A small man attached by a leash to a large Labrador dog looked round. 'Hell of a pong, eh?' he remarked with relish. 'Hell of a mess too. They say it went up like a torch.'

'So it would seem,' Joanna said drily.

The little man lowered his voice and jerked his head conspiratorially towards two men in dark suits, conferring over a file of papers. 'See them? They're from the insurance—loss adjusters. They've been here all afternoon. Bobbies all over the place too.' He winked. 'They reckon it weren't no accident. Someone was seen running away, seemingly.'

Joanna's heart missed a beat. 'Do they know who it was?'

'Couldn't say, I'm sure. That chap Blackstone would know. He's the one who spotted him.' He bent down to pat his dog. 'All right, old lad, I'm coming.'

Joanna bit back a gasp, as he wandered off. Cal had actually seen the arsonist, she thought frantically. But he'd said nothing about that at the house last night. Why ever not? She swallowed. Perhaps the police were setting a trap for Simon, and maybe Cal was afraid that she'd warn him—tell him to keep away.

I can't just wait for it to happen, she thought violently. The Craft Company is in ruins. I can't stand by and see the same thing happen to our lives.

She half ran back to the car.

It was the same receptionist at the country club. She looked at Joanna regretfully when she asked if she could see Mr Blackstone.

'I'm afraid he's not available, Mrs Bentham.'

'If he's busy, I'd be prepared to wait...'

The girl shook her head. 'You don't understand. Mr Blackstone has left for the day.'

'Already?' Joanna asked despairingly. 'It really is most urgent that I see him.'

The girl thought for a minute. 'Well, I do know where you'll find him,' she said. 'I'm not supposed to give it out, of course, but——'

'I'd be eternally grateful.'

'He's up at Nethercrag,' said the receptionist. 'He's just bought a house there. I've got the name somewhere...'

'It's all right.' Joanna summoned a smile. 'I—know what it is.'

Cal's car was parked outside the cottage when she arrived there. She walked up the path and knocked at the door, not giving herself time to think, to question the advisability of what she was doing, or change her mind.

He answered almost at once. His brows snapped together when he saw who it was.

She said, 'Don't send me away, please.'

'I wasn't considering it,' he said curtly. 'You'd better come in.'

The cottage smelled strongly of freshly applied paint, and there were spatters of the stuff on his elderly shirt and jeans.

'I wasn't expecting visitors.' He led the way into the sitting-room. 'Would you like some coffee?'

'Later, perhaps,' she said, and flushed under the sardonic glance he directed at her.

'So,' he said. 'To what do I owe the honour of this visit?'

She took a deep breath. 'I've just been down to the workshop. Someone said you'd—actually witnessed someone running away.'

'How news does get around,' Cal said drily. 'That's basically accurate, yes.'

'Have you told the police who you saw?'

'Naturally.' His frown deepened. 'What did you expect?'

'Nothing really,' she said with difficulty. 'I—hoped, perhaps, to persuade you to hold your hand—not to give him away, until we'd all had a chance to talk—to try and work something out.' She ran her tongue round her dry lips. 'I suppose he'll go to prison.'

'It's possible, but unlikely,' he returned. 'Why are you so concerned? I'd have thought you wanted him caught.'

'Want to see Simon destroyed?' she asked incredulously. 'Are you mad?'

There was a silence, deep and unbroken as if both of them had suddenly stopped breathing. Then,

'I think I must be,' Cal said slowly. 'What has Simon got to do with all this?'

She stared at him. 'Why—everything, I'd have thought.'

'What makes you say that?'

She ran the tip of her tongue round her dry lips. 'Well, it was Simon who you saw—wasn't it?'

'No,' he said. 'It was a vagrant called Tom O'Neill, better known locally as Paddy Tom. He likes comfort at night, so he prefers to break into buildings that are in use and doss down. He's been chased from every mill and industrial estate in the West Riding, I should think. He also likes a cooked supper, only last night his time-bomb of a stove finally exploded, and nearly cooked him as well. The police picked him up near Barnsley, still running.'

'Paddy Tom,' Joanna repeated. Suddenly she didn't know whether to laugh or cry. 'But I thought...'

'You thought Simon had developed a sideline in arson.' Cal's brows lifted in utter disbelief. 'Not very sisterly, or very flattering, especially when he's down in London trying to retrieve the Chalfont fortunes from my sinister clutches.'

'You know where Simon is?' Her voice was incredulous.

'Of course.' He sounded impatient. 'Although admittedly I'm not supposed to. He's talking to a friend of mine in a merchant bank about venture capital for the Craft Company.'

'How can you possibly know that?' Joanna sank down on to the sofa, feeling that her legs would no longer support her. 'You asked me where he was. You implied——'

'I put Jeremy in touch with him in the first place. But I wanted to check that Simon was following up the approach.' He paused. 'He doesn't know anything about my part in all this, of course, and it's essential he doesn't know.'

'But why?' She spread her hands helplessly. 'Why should you do that?'

'To let him off the hook. To release him from any sense of obligation to me. To provide the beginning of the end of this whole dreary bloody mess.' Cal spoke with a kind of weary distaste. 'It's gone on for too long—taken too much time and energy from all of us that could have been better spent. As I told you, I want it over with.'

'Yes.' She drew a deep breath. 'But—you see—when you said you wanted to see Simon urgently, I thought . . .'

'That I wanted to accuse him of burning down his business?' Cal shook his head. 'On the contrary, I was planning to offer him a temporary site on the mill complex while he rebuilds.' His mouth twisted. 'He'll almost certainly refuse, but I'll have made the gesture, and maybe, from now on, we can all get on with our own lives in peace.'

Peace? she thought. What peace can there be when I'm being torn apart like this? When your eyes don't meet mine? When you speak as if we're mere acquaintances, and there's no warmth in your smile? When you stay on the other side of the room?

She said unevenly, 'I seem to have made a major fool of myself, and I apologise. I was too upset to think clearly. I'd better go.'

'You'll have that coffee first.' Cal gave her a critical glance. 'You look like hell.'

She smiled pallidly. 'Ever the flatterer.'

When she was alone, she glanced round the room. Some of the furnishings, the sofas for instance, she recognised from the apartment at the country club. She remembered some of the ornaments too. And in its accustomed position beside the fireplace hung Joanna Chalfont's portrait.

He came back with a tray. She saw a cafetière, pottery beakers and a matching cream jug. He saw her looking, and smiled sardonically.

'It's all right—there are no unexpected additives this time, I promise. Although you still look as if you could do with a night's sleep,' he added frowningly.

'Is it any wonder?' She forced a smile in turn. She had to try for lightness, she decided, and impersonality, if that was possible. She glanced round brightly. 'So you decided to buy the cottage after all. I'm glad.'

'Thank you.' He poured the coffee and handed her a beaker. 'I decided it was time I had a proper home. The apartment was always temporary.'

'You didn't want to move into your family's house?' It was more like a mansion, she thought. Bigger and grander than Chalfont House in every way.

'That was never a home,' he said. 'It was a statement—a declaration of war, and I've finished with all that. I've had various offers from people wanting to turn it into a private school, or nursing home. Or it could be converted into flats. I'm in no hurry to decide.'

Joanna looked towards the fireplace. 'But you've still got the miniature.'

'Family heirloom,' he said. He leaned back in his seat. 'A gift of love.'

'Yes.' She paused. 'Cal—I found out the truth for myself. I wanted to tell you that. I know that they really loved each other. That she only stayed with Grandfather for my father's sake. And I suppose for the baby?' she added questioningly.

'The baby?' Cal's eyebrows lifted. 'Then you don't know all of it, Joanna.'

She bit her lip. 'I—wondered. It was something Daddy said.' She hesitated. 'You're telling me that it was Callum's child she was expecting, not Jonas's?'

'Of course it was.' His face was fierce suddenly. 'Don't judge them too harshly, Joanna. My grandfather was a widower, and lonely. Your grandparents hadn't shared a room, or much of a life, since your father's birth. Once Jonas had his son and heir, he assumed any decent woman would be thankful to be done with that kind of thing. He had women in the village he used when he felt the need.'

He sighed harshly. 'I suspect that being loved—being wanted was a revelation to her. She assumed, naïvely, that as Jonas no longer cared about her he would let her go once he knew the truth. But she misread the situation. When she told him she'd fallen in love with one of his employees and was pregnant by him, he nearly went mad. But it wasn't his marriage he was trying to preserve. It was his pride, his standing, his damnable self-importance. So he used the only weapon he had. He told Joanna if she left him, she would never be allowed to see her son again, and that he'd make the boy suffer for his mother's wickedness.'

Joanna shuddered. 'That's—monstrous!'

'Yes,' Cal agreed bleakly. 'No woman should be asked to cope with that kind of blackmail. To protect your father, she gave in. She saw Grandfather once more—to explain and say goodbye. It must have been sheer hell for them both. He promised her that as soon as he'd established himself, he'd come for her and take Anthony and the baby too. That he'd fight for them all through every court in the land if need be.' His mouth twisted. 'It never occurred to him, of course, that when he came back she'd have—gone, and their child with her.'

'And that was when he decided on revenge.'

'Yes.' Cal's face was sober. 'Jonas had robbed him of a future with the woman he loved. In turn, he'd take everything Jonas cared for. It was as simple as that.'

'I can understand now why your grandfather was so bitter—so implacable against our family.'

'He had the best of reasons. The mistake was to carry the bitterness down succeeding generations. I should have put a stop to it a long time ago.'

'Then why didn't you?'

Cal shrugged, his expression wry. 'Because, like my grandfather before me, I made the mistake of wanting a Chalfont woman, and to hell with the consequences. I should have settled for one of the girls who wanted me instead. Life would have been safer—easier that way.'

'Yes.' She could hear that awful brightness in her voice again. She drank the rest of her coffee and reached for her bag. 'Well, I'm sure it's not too late. You've never exactly lacked for female admirers.' Oh, God, I sound so hideously prissy! 'So it's a fresh start for both of us, and no recriminations.'

'I hope so.' As she rose, he got to his feet too. 'What are your immediate plans?'

'I haven't given them much thought as yet.' She summoned a smile. 'I'll probably go back to the States. I liked it there.'

'Why run?' he said. 'There's nothing to escape this time.'

Oh, yes, there is. The knowledge that you don't want me any more. That you'll never kiss me or touch me again. The reality of you living in this house, married to some rich man's suitable daughter.

She lifted her chin. 'And nothing to keep me here either.'

'Is that the truth?' he said. 'Tell me, Joanna, before I go on my knees to you and beg you to stay.'

Her heart seemed to stop. 'The joke is over,' she said unsteadily. 'You said so yourself.'

'I'm not joking, damn you!' He was deathly pale, a tiny muscle working beside his mouth. 'I bought this house, hoping and praying that it was for us both. I've dreamed of nothing else but you here beside me. I'm even using the other bedroom, because I don't want to sleep alone in that bed. When I wake up there, I want you, my wife, in my arms.'

He looked at her, and she saw there were tears in his eyes. 'What's past is done, Joanna. There's a lot we both have to regret, but that doesn't necessarily cancel the future. Don't go, my darling. Don't leave me. Because this time I'll follow, no matter how far it is.'

For a moment there was silence, then she took one uncertain step towards him. In the next instant she was in his arms, held so tightly, so passionately she could neither move nor breathe.

He said her name, his voice shaking, then he was kissing her deeply, and without restraint, and she was responding, her heart on her lips.

In between kisses, they spoke the first words of the love neither could bear to deny any longer. Half laughing, half crying, they reproached each other.

'I thought you didn't want me any more.'

'I thought I'd lost you forever.'

'Why didn't you tell me? Why did you never say...?'

'Would you have believed me?'

'I believe you now.'

'Yes.'

He said the word, and she repeated it as if it were a vow.

Cal gathered her up in his arms and sat down on the sofa, cradling her possessively against him as if he would never let her go.

'I've done this all wrong, of course,' he said, smothering the ghost of a laugh against her hair. 'The plan was to get the cottage exactly as I wanted it, then start courting you, very decorously, very seriously. I thought my only chance was to convince you that, whatever might have been said or done in the past, my intentions were now strictly honourable.'

'What made you realise that?' Joanna stroked his cheek with fingers that trembled.

'I think I'd always known it,' he said slowly. From the first time I saw you, all those years ago—a scared kid in the back of a large car. When we met again, as adults, I spotted you across the room at some party. I didn't realise who you were at first, but there was this instant recognition, which almost knocked me backwards. Here she is, I thought, the woman I've been waiting for. Then someone told me your name, and I felt as if my guts had been wrenched out.'

He laughed unsteadily. 'It seemed like life's supreme irony—to see the girl you wanted above all others, and find out she was totally out of reach. I had a couple of drinks and argued with myself. It was time the feud was over and I knew it. Whatever the rights and wrongs of the situation, honour had been more than satisfied, and maybe this would be a good way to start repairing the fences, I told myself.

'So I wangled an introduction, and you looked at me as if I'd crawled out from under a stone.' He groaned. 'It had taken a lot of courage to come over to you, and I felt as if I'd been publicly slapped for my efforts. So I decided if you wanted to play rough, it was all right with me. That whatever you began, I could finish, and that one day, no matter how long it took or what it cost, you were going to belong to me completely.'

He looked at her wryly. 'I didn't bargain for the fact that you were equally determined to keep me at bay. When you married Martin, I nearly went insane. Your wedding night was the pits of my entire life. I keep getting these pictures in my mind of the two of you together—him holding you, touching you as I wanted to do. I drank myself into a stupor trying to erase them.'

Joanna stirred restively in his arms. 'Cal——'

'Let me finish, darling, please. I came close to hating you then. But, all the same, something told me this wasn't the end of the story. I kept telling myself—wait. Don't get mad, get even.' He paused. 'Then, of course, Martin had his accident, poor bastard.'

'Cal.' Joanna's voice shook. 'There's something I've got to tell you—to confess.'

'There's no need.' His hand gently stroked the sudden rigidity of her shoulder and arm. 'Whatever you did, I was largely responsible for, and God knows I'm not proud of that.'

'No.' She laid a finger on his lips, silencing him. 'I've got to tell you. It's worse than you know.' She took a swift, painful breath. 'That was no accident. I—I killed Martin.'

There was a silence. Cal's brows lifted. 'Literally?' he asked in a matter-of-fact tone. 'What did you do to him—saw through the brakes on the car?'

'Of course not!' She was horrified. 'But I might as well have done.' There was another silence. She moistened dry lips with the tip of her tongue. 'You say you want to marry me, but I don't think that's ever going to be possible.'

'I agree it may not be easy at first. But both sides are going to have to learn to accept it. I'm damned if we're going to drag this feud into another generation.'

'It has nothing to do with the feud,' Joanna interrupted swiftly. 'It has to do with me—with the kind of person I am. I ruined Martin's life when I married him. I destroyed him.' Her hands twisted together, the knuckles white. 'I meant it all for the best. I wanted to be a good wife to him. Instead, I made him so wretched that he didn't want to live any more.'

'Who the hell told you that?'

'He did. And his aunt confirmed it.' She swallowed. 'I can't risk doing that to another human being. You must see that.'

Cal stared at her, his face suddenly grim. 'There's no danger of that.'

'You can't know that. I didn't know it when I married Martin. I thought I'd be able to make him happy—to make our marriage work, but I never could. And it was all my fault. I couldn't love him in the way that he wanted.' She hesitated. 'In—that way.'

'Are you trying to tell me you don't love me in that way either?' He spoke gently, but there was an agonised fierceness in his eyes.

'I don't know,' she said. 'I—just don't know. With Martin, I was hopeless—useless. Nothing I tried to do made any difference. I didn't know how to help him—how to reassure him. I felt so guilty anyway, knowing I'd married him without being properly in love. I'd thought I could pretend, at first anyway, but he guessed immediately. He accused me...' Tears rose hot and thick in her throat. 'It was dreadful—a nightmare that went on and on. And I couldn't make it stop.' Her voice died away.

Cal was gazing at her, horrified understanding dawning on his face. He said quietly, 'Joanna—are you saying that you and Martin never...? That you're still a virgin?'

She nodded convulsively. 'Night after night, I tried, but nothing was any good. He knew I didn't love him properly, and it—affected him—his manhood.'

'And that's the burden you've been carrying all this time? All that guilt—all that blame?' Cal shook his head. 'Oh, my sweet—my poor little love.'

'It was my fault,' she said intensely. 'When he went out that night, I knew he was in a desperate state. I should have stopped him.'

'I doubt whether you could have done.' Cal's face was grave.

'But I should have tried,' she insisted. 'I was just using him, and he knew it. The least I could have done was attempt to save him.'

'No, my darling.' Cal looked at her soberly. 'Martin, poor devil, was a tragedy waiting to happen. Remember my telling you that we were at school together? Well, there were question marks about him—about his masculinity—even then. When you announced your engagement to him, I told myself I must have been wrong, that we'd done him an injustice. Now I suspect we were right all along.' He kissed her quivering mouth very gently. 'Believe me, my darling, if you used him, you were certainly a lifeline as far as he was concerned.'

'I don't understand.' Joanna frowned in bewilderment. 'Are you implying that Martin was—was...?'

'Homosexual?' Cal supplied. 'Yes, I think he undoubtedly was, but not overtly. That was the pity of it all. For some reason, it was something he wasn't prepared to acknowledge, even to himself, maybe through family pressure. His aunt, after all, was a formidable woman with a closed mind. I think Martin made a conscious decision to deny his own nature, because he was afraid. He wanted to be straight, to shut the closet door and lead what he thought would be a normal life. Only he found it wasn't going to be that simple.'

He put a strand of hair tenderly back from her face. 'Your guilt about not loving him can have been nothing compared to what he felt when he was actually living with you, trying to be your husband, and failing. Marriage is an intimate relationship, mentally as well as physically. He must have been terrified that you would guess the truth. Eventually, there was nowhere left for him to hide.'

'Oh, my God!' Joanna shuddered, hiding her face on Cal's shoulder. 'If only I'd known! Maybe I could have helped.'

Cal shook his head. 'Only if you could have made him face up to the truth about himself, and I doubt if anyone could have done that. In the end, he found a different sort of courage to solve his problems.' He took her chin in his hand, making her look at him. 'But you, my precious girl, have got to stop blaming yourself. Martin chose his own path. Unfortunately it happened to cross yours just at the wrong moment, that's all.'

'But I can't just—write him off.'

'Nor can you let him shadow your entire future.' Cal's voice was firm. 'Your relationship was a tragic mistake, I agree, but you seem to forget it could just as easily have destroyed you, if you'd been in love with him.'

Her face was still troubled. 'But if I fail you too . . .'

'You won't.' His hand traced a tantalising path down her slim body from breast to thigh, and all her senses surged in excited, uncontrollable response and need. 'You see,' he told her gently, 'you're the other half of me.'

His arms tightened round her. 'The past has done too much harm already. So let's start looking forward instead. You and I, my love, are going to be quietly married by special licence just as soon as it can be arranged. If there's any music to face, then we'll cope with it together, after the wedding.'

'They may never accept it,' said Joanna. 'My father—Simon.'

'We'll give them every chance,' Cal promised. 'But it's time we thought about ourselves—our wishes—our feelings.' He paused. 'Where do you want to spend our honeymoon?'

She smiled up at him, lovingly, lingeringly, the last wistfulness fading from her eyes. 'Oh, somewhere quiet and romantic and not too far away, with a four-poster bed.'

'I know the very place,' he whispered, and kissed her.

WELCOME TO

The quintessential small town where everyone knows everybody else!

Finally, books that capture the pleasure of tuning in to your favorite TV show!

GREAT READING... GREAT SAVINGS... AND A FABULOUS FREE GIFT!

Each book set in Tyler is a self-contained love story; together, the twelve novels stitch the fabric of the community. The covers honor the old American tradition of quilting; each cover depicts a patch of the large Tyler quilt.

With Tyler you can receive a fabulous gift ABSOLUTELY FREE by collecting proofs-of-purchase found in each Tyler book. And use our special Tyler coupons to save on your next TYLER book purchase.

Join your friends at Tyler for the sixth book, SUNSHINE by Pat Warren, available in August.

When Janice Eber becomes a widow, does her husband's friend David provide more than just friendship?

Summer Reading At Its Best

In July, Harlequin and Silhouette bring readers the Big Summer Read Program. Heat up your summer with these four exciting new novels by top Harlequin and Silhouette authors.

SOMEWHERE IN TIME by Barbara Bretton
YESTERDAY COMES TOMORROW by Rebecca Flanders
A DAY IN APRIL by Mary Lynn Baxter
LOVE CHILD by Patricia Coughlin

From time travel to fame and fortune, this program offers something for everyone.

Available at your favorite retail outlet.

BSR